I0797064

Tales from Ondiran:

The Eye of Ksera

Sorceress for Hire

Sinta, Sorceress-Detective

The Misadventures of Thonir

The Court Sorcerers
(expected, 2025)

SEDIGITUS SWIFT

Sinta
Sorceress-Detective

Archelaus
Washington, DC

Published by *Archelaus*

archelaus-cards.com

This is a work of fiction. All of the characters and events portrayed in it are products of the author's imagination, as is Sedigitus Swift himself.

Cover art by Glen Evans

ISBN 978-1-961852-05-1 (paperback)
ISBN 978-1-961852-04-4 (ebook)

Sinta
Sorceress-Detective

Tales from Ondiran, Book Three

Dramatis Personae

Sinta, *a freelance sorceress*
Sir Othir, *her dashing man-at-arms*
Angvar, *her languid pet lizard*
Ferga, *her cook and housekeeper*

Lady Valdira, *Sinta's mentor*
Colmar, *her husband*
Haldor, *their son*

Prince Folgar, *ruler of the Principality of Sildoor*
Princess-Consort Mirelde, *his wife*
Sir Thanifor, *the prince's bodyguard*
Lady Mara, *the princess's confidante*

Sir Thennis, *long-serving chancellor of Sildoor*
Fothenar, *his faithful bodyguard*
Ghelnor, *his resourceful clerk*

Lord Alfron, *Gentleman of the Chamber (the first victim)*
Lady Hrinde, *his embittered widow*
Frildar, *their worthless son*

Halifor, *Court Sorcerer (the second victim)*

Lord Torvil, *Baron of Ferigan*
Lady Irolte, *his wife*
Lady Tisvena, *their daughter*

Lord Saafinor, *Baron of Toth*
Lady Siguldina, *his wife*
Lord Caador, *their son*
Lady Terinifulte, *their daughter*
Lord Anthilor, *their son*
Luria, *Anthilor's wife*

Lady Floria, *daughter of the Baron of Ninthan*

Lord Donaril, *unemployed son of the Baron of Hront*

Sir Thigtonil, *Lord Alfron's successor as Gentleman of the Chamber*

Sir Topassin, *Keeper of the Princely Seal*
Esmilinde, *his faithless wife*

Sir Rodor, *the prince's falconer*

Sir Rildan, *the prince's herald*
Drinna, *his wife*

Sir Hrogan, *Keeper of the Princely Library*
Fildenea, *his wife*

Sir Fainor, *first assistant to the treasurer*
Lady Tersa, *his wife and daughter of the Baron of Hront*

Thogril, *confidential secretary to the envoy from the County of Menfir*

Shingach, *the prince's chief cook*
Ghiron, *procurer of fresh produce for the castle*

Master Siv, *the public executioner*
Master Dvortin, *an alchemist*

an Inirochian assassin
a gang of thugs
a Lorventinian preacher

miscellaneous courtiers
sundry servants

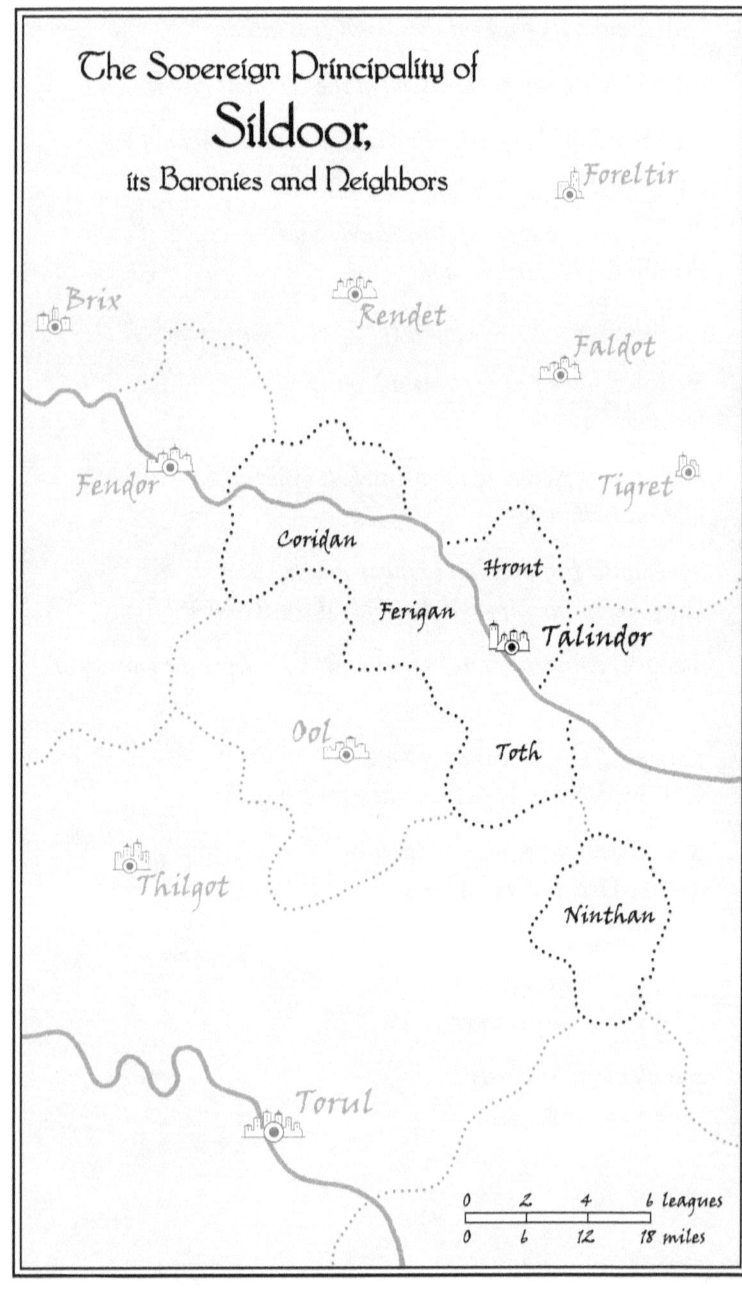
The Sovereign Principality of
Sildoor,
its Baronies and Neighbors
Foreltir
Brix
Rendet
Faldot
Fendor
Tigret
Coridan
Hront
Ferigan
Talindor
Ool
Toth
Thilgot
Ninthan
Torul
0 2 4 6 leagues
0 6 12 18 miles

1

For centuries prior to unification, the Ondiric Empire was little more than a notional hodgepodge of sovereignties, large and small, most of them Ondiric speaking, under a feeble imperial crown.

—*A Concise but Complete History of World Events*

Unfazed by the thick clouds blocking the light of the two moons, the lone figure in a hooded cloak moved with preternatural assurance through the darkness, while ascending the rugged western slope of the high hill. Upon reaching the castle at the top, the figure—in a remarkable display of free climbing that would have dismayed the structure's long-dead architects—exploited the shallow angle formed by the meeting of the curtain wall with a massive round tower to scale thirty feet of sheer stone in less than five minutes. Finding no guards atop this section of the battlements, the intruder quickly crossed to the other side and began a more challenging ascent of fourteen feet on a curving diagonal to a window on the eastern side of the tower. Although now in full view of much of the castle, the climber remained undetected—due in part to the cloudy night, but in part also to the chameleon-like qualities of the hooded cloak, which provided an effective magical camouflage against the mottled gray stone. Several tense minutes passed, as the intruder clung precariously to the side of the tower, while contriving to open the latched window without breaking it—or falling some forty feet to a bone-shattering death on the cobbles below.

Once inside, the hooded figure dropped lightly onto the wooden floorboards of the large workshop or laboratory that took up the entire eastern half of this level of the tower. The room was overflowing with esoteric objects and mysterious equipment, ranging from an enormous armillary sphere near the window to a fully articulated walrus skeleton with thirty-inch tusks by the door. Paying these interesting distractions no heed, the intruder instead maneuvered sure-footedly through the cluttered darkness to a ladder leading to an open trapdoor in the ceiling. Climbing it in something approaching silence proved difficult, but with time and care the intruder emerged successfully into a small but similarly crowded bedchamber.

It was a warm night, and the room's half-naked occupant had kicked off his bedclothes. In his mid-thirties, he was unexceptional in appearance. His slow, steady breathing confirmed that he was still asleep. The intruder approached and studied him dispassionately for a moment before drawing a long, narrow-bladed dagger and thrusting it with both force and precision between the fourth and fifth ribs, through the musculature of the intercostal space and the fibrous tissues of the pericardium, and into not only the left but also the right ventricle. A swift jerk freed the enchanted blade, while slicing open the punctured heart. Blood gushed from the wound, as the sleeper gasped and opened his eyes, awake and uncomprehending in the dark for just seconds before he succumbed to unconsciousness. Less than a minute later, he was dead.

With an indistinct vocalization, the killer dipped a finger in the blood and placed a single daub on the victim's forehead, before cleaning the dagger, returning it to its sheath, and making for the bedchamber window. There the clouds chanced to part for a moment, and the light of the larger of the two moons flooded in, illuminating for the first time the distinctive face concealed by the hooded cloak—angular, high-cheekboned, and female.

Evidently the cloak had more than one magical quality, for after taking hold of special handgrips sewn into the fabric and placing her feet in a pair of cloth stirrups, she leapt from the already open window, stretched out all four limbs, and glided forth like a flying squirrel. Banking sharply around the tower, she cleared the battlements of the curtain wall and swooped down the side of the hill to the bottom, thus effecting her escape.

2

Sildoor. One of several minor states to emerge from the Time of Troubles, the Principality of Sildoor comprises five mostly contiguous baronies in eastern Ondiran. Ruled by the House of Solint from the capital at Talindor, it is considered generally unremarkable.

—*The Great Ondiric Compendium of All Knowledge*

Sinta could not help laughing at Othir's slyly malicious tale of how, at age eight, he had tricked his trio of tyrannical aunts into spending an uncomfortable afternoon trapped in a henhouse. The attractive young sorceress and her dashing man-at-arms were in a buoyant mood, as they returned home to Talindor from a successful journey to the island kingdom of Tserenets. Sinta had acquired a rare authentic copy of *Djanko's Grimoire,* the masterwork of one of the great Tseren sorcerers (and the subject of many forgeries), while Othir had finally obtained a magic sword, albeit one that did not seem altogether to approve of him (as sometimes happens initially when such weapons change hands).

Leaving their horses at the livery stable, the two walked the short distance to the town square, where they found a member of the princely guard standing outside the apothecary's shop that Sinta had inherited three years earlier upon her father's death, and out of which she operated her freelance sorcery business. As they approached, she recognized him by sight as the man assigned to protect the prince's elderly chancellor. She also recognized the chancellor's arms on the caparison of the bay mare whose reins the man held.

Othir knew this person somewhat better. "Greetings, Fothenar. I hope Chancellor Thennis is not in need of medicaments!"

"No, Sir Othir," the soldier replied respectfully. "His Excellency wished to speak with Mistress Sinta." Stepping aside with a slight bow, he let them enter the shop.

"Ah, here they are now!" declared Pentigor, the master apothecary who rented the premises from Sinta.

The chancellor turned around with evident relief. "Thank goodness! Greetings to you both. Master Pentigor was not certain when you might return." He took a deep breath. "Mistress Sinta, I need your help in a confidential matter. Sir Othir, you may also prove to be of assistance, I think."

Sinta found the undertone of agitation she detected in the chancellor's voice disconcerting, for she knew him to be a man of calm authority, who had guided the fortunes of the tiny Principality of Sildoor with a steady hand since before she was born. Moreover, in her previous—though admittedly not extensive—dealings with him, the old man had invariably summoned her to his office in the castle; he had never come to look for her in person. Something serious must be afoot.

She invited him upstairs to her study. Othir followed with their bags, which he quickly stashed in their respective bedchambers, though not before Sinta extracted her pet lizard, Angvar, from his travel basket and placed him in the windowsill, where he could bask in the sun.

The chancellor sat gratefully down on the second-hand chair provided for Sinta's clients. He took a moment to catch his breath following the two flights of stairs. "Eight days ago," he then began, "Lord Alfron, acting as the prince's food taster, became ill while sampling the prince's dinner and died within minutes. Naturally, the prince was most alarmed at this apparent attempt on his life—as well as distressed at the loss of Lord Alfron, his long-time friend and confidant—and he demanded an immediate investigation. I assigned the task to Halifor, who, as court sorcerer and a man of intellect, seemed to me best suited to the task. He fed samples from the various dishes served at the dinner to several different dogs and established thereby that the prince's serving of pork tenderloin alone contained a potent toxin. He then sought to identify the culprit, and I think he must have been making progress, because—and I'm sorry to have to tell you this, Mistress Sinta, for I believe the two of you were close—this morning he was found stabbed to death in his bed."

Sinta gave a horrified gasp and clasped her hand to her mouth. She and Halifor had in fact enjoyed a brief love affair the year before, and they had remained friends afterward.

Chancellor Thennis politely bowed his head to give the sorceress a little privacy at what he could see was an emotional juncture. He waited a moment before continuing. "That brings me to the purpose of my visit, namely, to ask you to pick up the investigation where Halifor left off." He raised a hand to forestall the objection he could see springing to Othir's lips. "I am fully cognizant, Sir Othir, of the danger inherent in my request, but I have confidence in your ability to keep Mistress Sinta safe. Additionally, we shall make every effort to keep the assignment secret." He turned back to Sinta. "We can explain your presence at court by saying that you are under consideration for the post of court magician." He smiled wryly. "Which has the added virtue of being true."

Sinta struggled to master the flurry of conflicting emotions sweeping over her. The news of Halifor's murder was of course a severe shock, albeit one now contending with a vengeful desire to find out who had killed him (the desire to find things out being one of Sinta's defining characteristics, even under normal circumstances); nevertheless, the grim example of Halifor's fate prompted a natural fear for her own safety, should she accede to the chancellor's request (a fear aggravated by her lifelong tendency toward timidity, something she despised in herself and sought to quash); finally, she felt a guilty pricking of ambition at the prospect of professional advancement—for becoming a court magician at the age of just twenty-three (and as a woman, no less) would be a rare accomplishment, even in a minor court such as that of Sildoor.

The chancellor waited patiently for Sinta to say something. "So, will you do it?" he asked at last.

His voice shook Sinta out of her reverie. "Yes, Your Excellency. Yes, of course, I will." She paused, as her conscious mind suddenly caught up with the workings of her unconscious, which was already evaluating the evidence before her. "Was Lord Alfron the prince's only taster?" she asked.

The chancellor shook his head. "No, it was a duty he shared with the other Gentleman of the Chamber, Lord Fentimor, who now shares it with Lord Alfron's successor, Sir Thigtonil."

Sinta frowned. "But they must alternate based on some established schedule?"

"Oh, yes. Lord Alfron tasted on even-numbered days."

"And this was generally known?"

The chancellor shrugged. "It was no secret within the court."

Sinta nodded. "Then I think you can reassure Prince Folgar that this was not an attempt to assassinate him. If the killer knew who would be doing the tasting, Lord Alfron was the intended victim. It makes no sense to have used such a fast-acting poison otherwise. They are, in any case, quite rare and difficult to procure. The only non-magical one I'm familiar with can be extracted from fruit pits, but it's quite a laborious procedure. No, if the intention had been to kill the prince, any competent poisoner would have chosen a slower-acting agent, such as hemlock, or arsenic, or wolfsbane. Those are all easy enough to come by, and Lord Alfron's first symptoms would not have become apparent until it was too late to save the prince."

The chancellor eyed her shrewdly. "I knew I was right to come to you," he said. "Halifor came to the same conclusion—but not half so quickly."

Sinta blushed. "Well, to be fair, his father wasn't an apothecary."

3

Inspector Orpintor frowned fiercely at his eight assembled suspects. "There is, ineluctably, only one logical explanation of the evidence in this case," he declared. "The butler did it!"

—*The Murder in the Pantry: An Inspector Orpintor Mystery*

Although hampered by her inability to take pointers from the rich tradition of Ondiric detective fiction, as this lay several hundred years in the future, Sinta possessed a tidy mind that let her address an unfamiliar problem starting from first principles. She thus opted to begin her investigation by going to the castle to view Halifor's body. To her annoyance, Alfron's had already been cremated, in accordance with the strict rites of his Hrintic faith.

Thennis had his clerk, Ghelnor, escort Sinta and Othir to the cellar beneath the round tower, where the body now lay in cool subterranean darkness to preserve it from the heat of the day. Steeling herself to face her friend's lifeless form, Sinta cast a light spell on the ceiling. The sight of Halifor stretched out on a trestle table, though less horrible than she feared, was still distressing. She stood back and turned instead to Othir for guidance.

"You're the one with experience treating the human body like a side of beef. What do you make of it?"

Othir stepped forward and studied the damage to Halifor's torso. He gave a low whistle. "I see one wound from a single blow to the chest. A thin blade, I think, inserted with force between the ribs—almost certainly straight into the heart—and then pulled out with a punishing yank to one side. Not what I was expecting at all. It's not easy to stab a person in the heart. The organ's well protected. No, there are *much* surer ways to deliver a fatal wound. This took strength, skill, and a precise knowledge of anatomy." He shook his head. "Whoever did this chose to do it the hard way!"

Sinta took a reluctant step closer. "Why do you suppose that would be?"

Othir shrugged. "Because they could? I'd be surprised if this weren't the work of a professional assassin, who takes pride in a clean job. Halifor would have been dead before he knew what was happening."

Sinta sighed. "Poor Halifor. That's something, I suppose." Curiosity drew her another step closer. "What's that on his forehead?"

Othir bent over the corpse. "A daub of blood." He shook his head. "I don't know. A signature? Part of some sort of ritual? Both?"

Sinta shuddered. That Halifor had been murdered was bad enough, without any need for macabre flourishes.

Next on the sorceress's agenda was a visit to the scene of the crime. Since they could not be sure where exactly that was in the case of Lord Alfron, they began with Halifor's bedchamber. Unfortunately, they saw little that seemed pertinent, beyond the pattern of blood spatter, which confirmed—even to their untrained eyes—that the magician had sustained a single blow while lying in bed, presumably asleep.

Sinta had brought along a spell book, however, that contained some of the notes from her apprenticeship. She opened it to a page she had marked carefully with a dried oak leaf prior to leaving her study. "This spell is called 'Speaking Stones,'" she explained, "and it should let me witness what happened here last night." She then entered into an extremely long and complex incantation, accompanied by elaborate hand gestures, most of which involved touching the stones of the room's curving exterior wall. Once she had completed the spell, daylight disappeared for her, as did Othir and Ghelnor, and she saw the darkened chamber as it had been the night before. Carrying, as she always did, an enchanted moonstone that gave her excellent night vision, she had no difficulty making out the defenseless figure of Halifor, asleep on his bed. A faint creaking noise drew her attention to the open trap door from which the hooded figure slowly emerged into view. Sinta watched with distress as the crime unfolded, helpless to stop it. Even with night vision, however, she was unable to get a good look at the killer's face until the last moment, when the moon broke through the clouds.

Sinta stood in the dark for a moment, trying to regain her composure—which seemed easier to do, somehow, when she could not see Othir and Ghelnor, even though she knew they could still see her. She ended the spell. "The killer is a woman," she told them, "and surely a professional assassin—at any rate, every bit as good with a dagger as you suspected, Othir." She carefully recapitulated what she had seen, both to apprise the others and to help preserve every detail in her memory. "I only got one good look at her face, but she appeared to be a southerner, perhaps an Inirochian. She had a remarkable magic cloak. When she wasn't moving, I could barely make her out. She was not invisible, but her cloak blended in very effectively with its surroundings." She looked out the window and down to the ground. "That must be a fifty-foot drop, but wearing that cloak she didn't hesitate to jump for a second."

Since the killer had entered via the trap door, Sinta and her companions descended to the floor below. The sorcerer's workshop had a vaguely metallic odor that Sinta had always found unpleasant. She repeated her spell to see what more she might learn there, but this time she did not have much to tell the others. "She got in by the window, which was closed and latched."

Othir examined the mechanism. "That can't have been easy."

Sinta sighed. "No, it did take her awhile. But poor Halifor made it easier for her by failing to enchant the window with an alarm or a trap." She shook her head sadly, having learned early in her apprenticeship that it was unwise to assume a point of entry need not be protected just because it might be difficult to access. "This woman can see well in the dark," she added, "for she had no trouble getting to the ladder without tripping on some of this stray clutter and falling flat on her face." Sinta shook her head again; she and Halifor had never seen eye to eye on the importance of an orderly workroom. She thought for a moment. "Also, she didn't take anything with her from either room, so if Halifor made any notes regarding his investigation, they should still be here."

They spent a good hour searching both chambers, as well as Halifor's study on the upper floor, without finding anything that seemed pertinent (though Othir did turn up a feminine undergarment an embarrassed Sinta recognized as her own).

Disappointed, they moved on to search Alfron's suite of rooms, located in the castle's primary structure, near the prince's own chambers. They were not sure what exactly they expected to find there, but as Othir pointed out, if Alfron had been involved in something shady that led to his death, there was no telling where the evidence of his corruption might lead them. Fortunately, Alfron's embittered widow, Hrinde, one of the princess-consort's ladies-in-waiting, had her own rooms elsewhere, so they could conduct their search uninterrupted and without jeopardizing the secrecy of their investigation.

"I would take a close look at Lady Hrinde, if I were you," suggested Ghelnor, obviously glad to have some potentially useful information to impart. "She and Alfron detested one another. The only way they could both remain in the same court was for each to pretend the other didn't exist—but that must have been hard going for her, given his frequent ill-concealed affairs."

Indeed, evidence of Alfron's infidelities quickly came to light, in the form of a sizeable wicker hamper filled with love notes, perfumed handkerchiefs, and other erotic souvenirs, some presumably dating back years. Sinta counted twelve different handwritings on the notes, but most of the senders had not signed them, on the perhaps optimistic theory that Alfron would surely not have more than one paramour at a time and would thus know who penned them. Others closed their missives with various nauseating pet names, such as Snookums, Wee Baa-Lamb, and Your Little Cabbage Dumpling. The notes thus provided no transparent clues as to the identities of their authors. Sinta nevertheless took custody of them—albeit with a distinct lack of enthusiasm—in case they should prove important later. "We appear to have no shortage of potential suspects already," she remarked with a sigh, "from his aggrieved wife to possible jilted lovers and presumably angry cuckolds."

"I suspect Goo-Goo Baby Doll," said Othir with disgust. "Just on principle."

By this time it had gotten late. Sinta thanked Ghelnor for his help. "You can tell the chancellor that we have made progress," she added, "and that I have a plan to find Halifor's assassin. Othir and I will be traveling to Fendor tomorrow to pursue it."

Othir knew that Sinta's mentor, the renowned sorceress Valdira, lived in Fendor, the capital of the Principality of Fendoran, but he refrained from asking Sinta about her plan as they walked home, trusting her to tell him when she saw fit.

"Let's sleep on what we've learned today," Sinta suggested, as they crossed the square to the apothecary's shop. "We can discuss the matter tomorrow."

4

Like neighboring Ool and Sildoor, the Sovereign Principality of Fendoran is a small jurisdiction of little consequence, though a few tin mines operate in the south and the capital city of Fendor is home to several small merchant banks.

—*An Historical, Geographical, and Oeconomical Dictionary, Being an Instructive Miscellany of Information Useful to a Man of Business*

The next morning, Sinta and Othir sat down to a heavy breakfast of porridge, fried eggs, and salt-cured pork, served with small beer—all courtesy of Ferga, Sinta's cook and housekeeper, who firmly believed her employer was too petite for her own good. Sinta ate listlessly, however, and said little, having spent a restless night brooding on the loss of Halifor. Although their affair had lasted only a few months, and several of the man's more ingrained habits and mannerisms had gotten on her nerves, she had been fond of him, for he was a kind man, a good listener, and an adventurous cook, who also knew how to make her laugh. Sinta happened to have a particularly strong visual memory, and the image of his pale body on that trestle table in the cellar kept coming back to her with a vividness that was most unwelcome, particularly at breakfast-time.

"It will be good to see Valdira and Colmar again," observed Othir, hoping to lift Sinta's spirits. He did not approve of many people, but he liked Valdira and her husband.

Unable to disagree, Sinta nodded.

"Little Haldor must be old enough now to have started acquiring some vaguely human characteristics," Othir suggested.

"I suppose so," Sinta replied dubiously. She consulted her memory. "He should be two, I think." Sinta and Othir were not, either of them, extravagantly fond of babies.

Ferga, whose views regarding these creatures were more conventional, set another plate of pork down on the table with a disapproving thud. "Hmmph!" she snorted. "Sometimes I think it's the two of you who are only vaguely human."

At the livery stable, Sinta saddled her gentle chestnut rouncey, Tamirandalia, while Othir readied his spirited gray courser, Serifol. Having just returned from a long journey the day before, neither animal displayed enthusiasm at the prospect of a new departure, but both were fond of their owners and therefore willing to put up with a certain amount of their foolishness.

The heat of the previous days had moderated, and the weather promised to be pleasant, but Sinta remained moody and withdrawn for most of the morning, as they rode up the picturesque Vassata River valley toward Fendor. She perked up slightly at the prospect of lunch, however, at a roadside tavern she knew well. Not only would the food be good, but she could count on a nice discount, as the proprietress remained grateful to her for having cast a spell banishing rats and mice from the premises.

The tavern was bustling with tipsy Cantiferian pilgrims, pausing on their way downriver to a holy site on the coast. (Of Ondiran's four major religious traditions, Cantiferianism placed the greatest emphasis on pilgrimage, with its attendant opportunities for merrymaking.) Also present were two prosperous-looking merchants and their fierce-looking bodyguard, who were settling up their bill prior to continuing on their journey, as well as a weather-beaten forester in buckskin, who was chatting up a pretty waitress prior to ordering his meal. The proprietress spotted Sinta and Othir as they entered and personally conducted them to a table in a smaller adjoining room, away from the Cantiferians. After the briefest of intervals, she brought out a loaf of black bread, a platter of smoked sausages, and a pot of mustard, along with a stein of hopped beer for Othir and a glass of sweet cider for Sinta. All of these they consumed in appreciative silence for some minutes.

"Valdira owns a crystal ball," Sinta finally informed Othir, as she speared the last sausage with her knife, "and now that I know what the assassin looks like, I can use it to find her." She paused to devour the sausage. "It would be easier if I also knew her name, but her face will do."

The pilgrims began singing a lively song about monks and their alleged erotic preferences.

Othir finished his beer and suggested departure. "I think I already know all I care to concerning the monastic orders."

❦

The road improved as they crossed into the Principality of Fendoran, which had somewhat more tax revenue than Sildoor to expend on such luxuries. "Obviously, we're hoping that finding the assassin will get us to the bottom of both murders," Sinta observed. "But I think we ought to examine our underlying assumptions all the same. Should we be assuming that the two deaths are actually connected, when the methods of killing are so different?"

"It would be quite a coincidence, if they weren't connected somehow," Othir pointed out. "The princely court hasn't seen a murder in years—certainly not while we've been in Talindor. Now, suddenly, not only do we have two, but the victim of the second murder was investigating the first one."

"I agree it's very suspicious," Sinta conceded. "Thennis thinks there's a connection, and he's no fool. But I can't see the assassin who stabbed Halifor doing double duty as a poisoner. Why wouldn't she have just stabbed Alfron, too?" She frowned. "So, if our theory is that Halifor's investigation panicked whoever poisoned Alfron into hiring an assassin, then the question is, why? Why not just kill Halifor themselves?"

Othir considered the question for a moment. "I suppose the logical explanation is that an accomplished court sorcerer is a harder target than a philandering court flunkey. Halifor never struck me as stupid."

"No, he certainly wasn't, and in a case like this he would surely have taken precautions against being poisoned. He knew spells that would have protected him. And for all we know, the murderer might have hired the assassin only after trying and failing to kill Halifor themselves." Sinta flicked her wand at a large horsefly that had alighted ill-advisedly upon a vein in Tamirandalia's neck. The insect fell to earth with a slight sizzling sound. "No, we've got a working theory. I just think we shouldn't lose sight of the possibility that it might be wrong."

It was late afternoon before the travelers arrived in Fendor and rode to an imposing house in the most affluent district of the city. The only child of a baron, Valdira had inherited the elaborate structure upon his death, while his title and country estate passed to a male cousin. No mere idle aristocrat, she was a sorceress of great power and fierce intellect, not to mention considerable beauty, whom Sinta loved and revered, while also finding her, even now, ever so slightly terrifying. Fortunately, Valdira was always pleased to see her former apprentice, in whose growing success in Talindor she took justifiable pride.

To be sure, Valdira's cook grumbled a little at being obliged to accommodate two more for supper on short notice, but as she liked Sinta (and nurtured an enduring crush on the absurdly handsome Sir Othir), she did not really mean it.

The meal took place in the servants' dining hall, according to Valdira's established practice, with the entire household assembled, notwithstanding a slight delay occasioned by the late arrival of Valdira's husband, Colmar, together with her six men-at-arms. An old campaigner (though at thirty-nine he was hardly ancient), Colmar had taken them on an eight-hour field exercise that had stretched to nine. Valdira chided him, both for being late and for bringing everyone home with muddy boots, but she did not actually mind, having used the time to catch up with Sinta and subject her to little Haldor (who had, in fact, become more recognizably human since Sinta last saw him, being able to speak in complete—if still primitive—sentences now). For his part, Colmar was duly apologetic, pointing out that he would have taken pains to be more punctual had he known they had company. He and Sinta had a long-standing friendship, which began with his having once saved her life.

After supper, the two sorceresses retired upstairs to consult the crystal ball. Valdira retrieved it, along with the brass ring upon which it rested, from a locked cabinet in her study and placed them both on her oaken desk, clearing away several loose parchments, a large onion, a cracked ceramic dish, and a few Fendoric farthings to make room. The ring was engraved with symbols from the mystical language of sorcery, attributing the enchantment of the magic crystal to a practitioner named Ksiltefara, during the reign of Thigvor the Magnificent. If true, the artifact was nearly eight hundred years old.

Although Sinta had learned to use the device, she had never warmed to it, being unable to forget that the previous owner had employed it to abduct her and hold her hostage for the most miserable day and a half of her young life. She had no qualms, however, about using it now not only to find the assassin but perhaps to capture her, as well, by the very same method. She had therefore made a point of bringing her newly acquired copy of *Djanko's Grimoire,* which contained a teleportation spell. *Thou canst transporte onely that thou canst perceive,* she recalled her erstwhile abductor—a skeletal six-century-old sorceress—explaining, *and by this Orb perceivest thou what lieth a-farre.* She placed the grimoire on the desk in front of the crystal ball. It was a fine volume, bound with rich leather covers, silver clasps, and a narrow red ribbon for use as a bookmark. She opened it to the teleportation spell and took out her wand. "Almost ready," she told Valdira, who got out her own wand as a precaution, in case the captured assassin proved fractious.

Sinta took a deep breath. The combination of spells she was about to cast would be difficult, requiring the utmost concentration. She began with the incantation to activate the crystal ball's capacity to find someone (rather than to surveil a location or divine the future). The orb immediately clouded over, as though filled with turbulent fog. She quickly closed her eyes and cast a remembering spell that brought the assassin's face back to her with cinematic clarity. An exclamation of several syllables conveyed to the crystal ball that this face belonged to its target. Sinta reopened her eyes and watched, as the swirling fog slowly cleared, revealing a nondescript loft, in which her quarry was performing some rather extreme stretching exercises that looked painful. Sinta frowned. She had studied the teleportation spell the night before, but she had never cast it, and there was much more to using magic than mindlessly repeating an incantation or two, particularly at this level of complexity. She pointed her wand at the image in the crystal ball and began.

"Damnation!" she cried several minutes later, vexed by the anticlimax of the spell's failure to produce the desired result. "It didn't work."

"The woman probably has some sort of protection against hostile magic," suggested Valdira sensibly. "From what you've told me, it wouldn't be surprising."

"Either that, or I botched the spell." Sinta blushed with shame at having failed before her mentor.

"Oh, yes, very likely," scoffed Valdira, still watching the crystal ball. The assassin finished her stretches, picked up her dagger, and practiced an elaborate series of twirling tricks with it. "Pull back," Valdira instructed. "Let's see where we are."

Sinta gestured at the crystal ball and murmured several words in the mystical language of sorcery. The view zoomed out, up through the rafters and out above the roof. Sinta and Valdira both leaned in to examine the cityscape thus revealed. Fortunately, the summer days were long, and there was still some lingering twilight.

"Looks like Torul in the County of Menfir," Valdira said after a moment.

"Yes, you're right. I recognize that Asardian high temple," Sinta confirmed, pointing. "Torul's about two days' ride, isn't it?"

Valdira smiled. "Or less than three hours in the flying wagon!"

5

Torul in the historic County of Menfir is worth a detour for its medieval architecture alone. The Asardian high temple is a particularly fine example of the early Osfanic style. Racing enthusiasts will wish to visit the new autodrome just outside the city limits.

—*The Motor-Tourist's Guide to Ondiran* (3rd ed.)

The flying wagon was precisely what the name suggested—a wagon enchanted to fly. Valdira had borrowed it a number of years earlier from a Tseren friend who had always found it difficult to say 'no' to her, and what with one thing or another, she had never quite gotten around to returning it. Although the vehicle had an unimpressive, rustic appearance, it was extremely useful, as well as fun to fly, and she was inordinately fond of it.

Valdira took for granted that she and Colmar would accompany Sinta and Othir to Torul, indeed that she should take charge of the operation. "We'll leave without delay," she told Sinta, as they headed back downstairs to find Colmar and Othir. "We don't want to give that woman time to wander off."

Sinta nodded, content for the moment to let Valdira lead. "That's true. Besides, by arriving in the middle of the night, we'll stand a better chance of catching her by surprise—or even asleep."

To be sure, before they could leave, Valdira first had to put Haldor to bed, give certain instructions to the housekeeper, and assure the cook that they would be back in time for breakfast. Given the brevity of the planned trip, the party would travel light. Sinta carried a quarterstaff with her almost everywhere she went, along with a magic knife, so naturally she brought both. (Colmar had taken it upon himself to train her to use a staff for self-defense, and he had given her this particular one as a gift upon completing her apprenticeship. It had stood her in good stead in the intervening years.) Valdira never carried a weapon, but she brought along the crystal ball, which they were sure to need again once they got to Torul, and of course both sorceresses brought their wands. Colmar and Othir both had magic swords, even if Othir's still showed signs of resenting his possession of it. All four had magical devices that let them see in the dark. Othir's was in the form of a ring that also gave him the ability to move stealthily—albeit within limits since, like Colmar, he was wearing armor.

Valdira and Sinta sat at the front of the wagon, while the two men stretched out in back. The contraption was not particularly comfortable, but once aloft it usually gave a smooth ride. Valdira took hold of a sort of steering bar fastened to the front, and the vehicle obligingly rolled out of the townhouse's stable and into the courtyard. She then pressed down hard on the bar, and the wagon rose rapidly into the cool night air. Once it had cleared the roof, she steered hard to the left and accelerated fast toward the city's southern gate. "I'm afraid we'll have to stick to following the road," she said. "It will take a little longer than flying direct, but we don't want to get lost."

Sinta had stashed her quarterstaff in back, knowing that she would want both hands free to clutch the wooden seat beneath her in a death grip. She had always found Valdira's brisk approach to flying the wagon alarming. Colmar, on the other hand, just closed his eyes and tried to get some sleep, while Othir, who had never ridden in a flying wagon before, sat up and watched with interest as the countryside sped by below, silver-gray in the double moonlight. The larger of the two moons was nearly full, while the smaller was waxing gibbous, so together they provided an admirable amount of light, and Othir's ring let him see even better.

Fendoran was a relatively prosperous principality with well-tended fields and good pasture land. The wagon flew over several villages, skirted a small castle, and passed a tin mine, before traversing the significant stretch of woodland that separated Fendoran from the much larger County of Menfir. Reaching a substantial town, Valdira took the wagon higher, so as to avoid the taller buildings. Lights were visible twinkling faintly in a few of the more affluent residents' windows. Before long, however, the wagon had rejoined the road to Torul, which passed further features of interest, including a glistening silver lake dominated by an impressive castle perched atop a small rocky island.

Eventually, their destination hove into view. Once they had cleared the city walls, Valdira and Sinta began a painstaking comparison of such features as the count's palace and the Asardian high temple, as seen through the crystal ball, with their view of them from the flying wagon. Othir woke Colmar—somewhat prematurely, as it turned out, for he had not realized that it would take nearly half an hour to find the warehouse they were looking for. That the building itself was excessively nondescript, resembling many similarly nondescript structures in its general neighborhood, did nothing to help the process along, but eventually the two sorceresses agreed that they had found it, and Valdira set the wagon down quietly in the alley behind.

Sinta decided it was time to take command of the operation. She pointed to the building's rear gable, thirty feet above their heads, where the loft had a loading door, serviced by a cantilevered roof beam and an empty pulley. "That's how Othir and I are going in. Valdira, you'll take us up in the wagon. Colmar, once we're inside, you'll cut off the assassin's escape by going in through the back door and blocking the stairs. She's asleep and appears to have the whole warehouse to herself. You shouldn't meet anyone, but that doesn't mean she hasn't devised defenses of her own against intruders. So, be on your guard."

Colmar nodded. "Indeed. The plan appears sound, as far as it goes."

For her part, Valdira accepted the role of elevator operator without demur, content to watch her former apprentice in action.

With a rush of adrenalin compensating for her lack of sleep, Sinta accompanied Colmar to the back door, which she tapped with her wand. Detecting no magic, she cast a spell to unlock it. "Good luck!" she whispered, before returning to the wagon and climbing in back with Othir. "Take us up," she told Valdira, who pressed down on the steering bar. The wagon rose quickly to the desired height, and Sinta tested the loading door for magic. Finding none, she unlocked it, as well, and stood back with her staff, as Othir pulled it open and stepped into the darkened loft.

6

Little is known for certain about the assassins' guild in medieval Ondiran, as its records, if they survive, have never been found. Its deadly membership is understood always to have been small, but dispersed throughout the Empire, and its bylaws are rumored to have been strict.

—*The Encyclopædia Ondiricana* (12th ed.)

A cloud of finely ground black pepper enveloped Othir, invading his eyes and nose. There may not have been any magical traps on the loading door, but the assassin had still rigged up a simple mechanical one. Black pepper was expensive, for profit-minded Inirochian merchants held a monopoly on its importation, but the spice proved its worth in this instance, throwing Othir into a paroxysm of sneezing. Just behind him, Sinta sneezed once, as well, though at least she did not get any pepper in her eyes. Downstairs, Colmar encountered what should have been an even noisier trap, when a bucket of rusty nails and other bits of old junk emptied upon his head. He was wearing a magic ring, however, that conveniently diverted missiles of all sorts, including descending chunks of scrap metal, onto another plane of existence. A few pieces that would have missed him anyway clattered to the floor, but most of the load simply vanished.

A light sleeper, the assassin rolled nimbly out of bed and snatched up her weapons. Before Othir could stop sneezing, she had hurled a throwing knife at him, though it failed to penetrate his hauberk, due in no small part to the protective enchantments Sinta had applied during the armor's manufacture. A second knife followed, this one directed at Sinta, who made use of her self-defense training to throw herself on the floor and roll further inside the room. As a result, the knife missed and lodged in the wooden doorframe with a loud thwack.

Knowing the woman likely had some form of protection against hostile spells, Sinta made no attempt to cast one at her directly. Instead, she conjured a heavy fisherman's net, some twelve feet in diameter, on the ceiling and let gravity do the rest.

Caught in the net, the assassin lost her balance and fell to the floor, where she struggled unsuccessfully to free herself, while loosing an angry stream of profanity that no one else in the room had Inirochian enough to understand.

"Lie still and be quiet, you murdering bitch," Sinta shouted, "or I'll beat you black and blue with my staff!" She looked out the door and saw the flying wagon still hovering outside. "Land the wagon," she told Valdira, "and come on up." She saw that Othir, though no longer sneezing, still appeared more or less incapacitated by the pepper in his eyes. "And bring the waterskin."

Colmar soon reached the top of the stairs, followed after a bit by Valdira. Colmar then guarded the prisoner, while the two sorceresses helped Othir flush the irritant from his eyes. The latter task accomplished, they turned their attention to their captive, who still clutched her long, narrow assassin's dagger in one hand, albeit immobile under the heavy net.

Sinta prodded her in the back with her staff. "Let go of the dagger."

Colmar pressed the tip of his sword to the woman's throat. "Do as she says!"

Reluctantly, the prisoner released her grip. "Who are you people?" she demanded. She spoke Ondiric with the studied precision of someone who has worked hard to master a second language, though she retained a telltale Inirochian accent that exaggerated Ondiric long vowels.

Sinta prodded her in the back again. "We're the ones asking the questions here. But since you're interested, we're friends of Halifor, the sorcerer you killed in Talindor two nights ago."

The prisoner shrugged her shoulders indifferently. "Oh, him. That was a clean kill. Fully according to guild rules. You have no quarrel with me. Your quarrel is with the client."

Sinta refrained from prodding her a third time. "You come very readily to the point. Who was this client? With whom is our quarrel?"

The prisoner shrugged again. "I don't know. The guild protects the name of the client, even from the operative assigned. Always. It is an important part of the service."

Unsure whether to believe her, Sinta decided on a new approach. "Valdira, help me search her. Colmar, you keep that sword to her throat. Othir, you hold onto her feet." Reaching through the meshes of the net, she and

Valdira patted down the prisoner, who was wearing nothing more than a shift in any case, and removed a ring and an amulet. Hoping thus to have relieved her of any possible magical protections, Sinta cast a charm spell. "Who was the client?" she demanded, touching the side of her nose.

The prisoner grimaced, as she struggled against the spell. Evidently she overcame it, for she replied by inviting Sinta to perform unnatural acts with troll spawn.

Resisting charm spells is a matter of practice and mental discipline, but it also depends on how much magical power the caster puts into the spell. Realizing that a trained assassin was likely to be a hard case, Sinta had applied more power than usual, but Valdira now stepped up to give it a try instead. She carried an ancient artifact that gave her access to a vast reservoir of magical power, upon which she now drew to throw a charm spell of such overwhelming force that the prisoner's muscles went slack and her eyes rolled back briefly in her head.

"Tell the truth. Who was the client?"

The prisoner struggled to focus.

"Who was the client?" Valdira repeated.

The prisoner gave a low moan. "I don't know."

Sinta seethed with frustration. "What about the death of Lord Alfron by poisoning? Do you know anything about that?"

"Answer truthfully," Valdira commanded.

The prisoner shook her head weakly. "Nothing."

Sinta groaned, her hopes for a quick conclusion to the investigation having evaporated. "Well, damn it, that's that. I suppose there's nothing left for us to do now except take this creature back to the authorities in Talindor." She paused, having remembered something else she wanted to know. "Tell me, why did you daub blood on Halifor's forehead?"

The prisoner's words came haltingly. "I was … saying … a prayer … for his soul."

Restraining herself with difficulty from striking the helpless woman with her staff, Sinta sought an outlet for her feelings regarding this sort of cold-blooded piety by kicking a nearby crate instead, but it was heavier than it looked, and she hurt her toe. She hobbled a few steps away. "Well, I don't plan on saying one for yours, when they hang you!"

Vengeful though Sinta might have been feeling at the moment, she had to admit that it was only fair to let the prisoner get dressed before they left for Talindor. She and Valdira carefully examined a linen kirtle they found hanging on the wall and a sturdy pair of shoes they found on the floor, to make sure they neither possessed magical qualities nor held concealed articles. Sinta then dispelled the fisherman's net and let the woman get up and put them on. Colmar took custody of the dagger and retrieved the two throwing knives, before joining Othir in a search of the loft for anything else of interest. Apart from the sheaths for the weapons, however, all they found was a coin purse holding some small change and a ceramic jar filled with gold pieces of various sizes and points of origin.

Colmar had just finished tying the prisoner's hands with a length of cord he had shown the foresight to bring along, when she suddenly tensed her muscles and shook her head.

"You're making a big mistake," she warned.

Valdira raised her eyebrows. That this woman should already have managed to break such a powerful charm was a remarkable feat.

Sinta rapped the floorboards with the burnished iron tip of her quarterstaff. "And just what exactly makes you think so?" she demanded.

The prisoner shrugged. "Two reasons. First, you have no proof I've killed anyone. Turn me in, and I'll just accuse you of bearing false witness against me. They'll put both of us to the torture in order to extract a confession." She smiled grimly. "Who do *you* think will break first?"

Despite herself, Sinta shuddered. She had been tortured before, albeit never by the judicial authorities, so she had no foolish illusions on the subject. "And the second reason?"

The assassin drew herself up to her full height. "Guild law. Had you apprehended me in the course of my assignment, that would have been on *me.* You would have been well within your rights either to kill me on the spot or clap me in irons for the pleasure of the public executioner. But you didn't. I got away clean. That is on *you.* Bring about my death now, and the guild will see to it that you do not survive my demise by many days. As I told you before, your quarrel is with the client, whoever that person may be. I am just a neutral instrument."

Though Sinta had no prior experience with the assassins' guild, she felt an odd conviction that the woman was telling the truth about its rules. This time she knew better than to express her feelings by kicking anything. Perplexed, she looked to the others.

Colmar frowned. "I think she's just played the high card. The assassins' guild is no joke."

Valdira shook her head sadly. "I'm sorry, child. He's right, I'm afraid."

Othir gave her a thin smile. "What can I say? Ruthless, deadly, and generally one step ahead: the woman was born to be an aunt." Othir's upbringing had biased him irretrievably against the forces of auntdom.

Sinta turned back to the assassin with bitter resignation. "All right. We won't hand you over for investigation and trial. But I'll be damned if I let you pay no price at all for killing Halifor." She gestured expansively to the various items she and her friends had seized. "All your magical property is forfeit." She frowned. "Speaking of which, where's that cloak of yours gotten to?" She cast her eyes over the wall where she and Valdira had found the kirtle, until she spotted the garment hanging on a hook, masterfully blending itself in with the rough-sawn wood behind. "Ah, there it is." She took it, folded it up, and handed it to Valdira. "And we're confiscating your weapons. You'll have to re-outfit yourself completely before you can undertake any more assignments." She stepped over to look the assassin straight in the eye. "How much were you paid for this last one? Tell me the truth, or I'll ask that nice lady to charm you again. Last time you didn't appear to find the experience enjoyable."

The assassin made a face. "Sixteen Sildooric princely crowns. Before expenses."

Sinta took the ceramic jar from Othir and opened it. "Your expenses are your problem." There were in fact sixteen Sildooric crowns at the top of the stash. She counted them out. "These are going to charity," she said. "If there were a Benevolent Society for the Destruction of the Assassins' Guild, they would go to that, but since there isn't, they will go as alms to the poor." She dropped the jar with its remaining contents onto the woman's straw-filled bedsack, and Othir followed her lead by tossing the coin purse onto it, as well. Sinta turned once again to the assassin. "One more question: where would the client have gone to commission the assassination? Does the guild have representation in Talindor, or would the client have had to travel?"

The assassin was silent for a moment, perhaps considering whether answering this question would violate guild rules. "They could have come here to Torul," she said, "or they could have gone to Faldot in the Duchy of Mar-Faldot. Those would be the closest places."

Sinta looked to Valdira. "I think we're ready to leave. Would you please go downstairs and get the flying wagon? I think we should exit the same way we came in."

Colmar was the last one to step out the loading door back into the wagon. Just before he did so, he whispered to the assassin: "Consider yourself lucky to have gotten off so lightly. But know that if you make any trouble for that young woman with the guild, my good wife will settle accounts with you—finally, definitively, and without leaving a trace!"

7

Under the House of Solint, the princely court in Sildoor grew over the centuries from a small, purposeful body in the early medieval period to a bloated, ineffectual organ of state power by the time of unification.

—*Form and Function: An Administrative History of the Predecessor States of the Province of Sindegorn*

There was little conversation during the flight back. Exhausted after the better part of two sleepless nights, Sinta stretched out in back alongside Othir, while Colmar sat up front with Valdira. By the time the flying wagon set down in Fendor, the first signs of twilight were becoming apparent, as the upper atmosphere scattered and refracted the light of the sun during the latter's slow ascent to the horizon. Following a sturdy breakfast, the four staggered up to their beds and slept until close to noon.

After lunch a brief meeting took place to divide the assassin's confiscated property. Othir received her dagger (thus giving him a second magic weapon that regarded him with suspicion). Colmar took the two excellent throwing knives with the intention of awarding them to whichever man in Valdira's small guard force demonstrated the greatest facility with their use. Sinta claimed both the amulet, which had protected the assassin from hostile spells, and the ring, which had endowed her with both night vision and stealth. Since she no longer needed the enchanted moonstone she had been using for night vision up to that time (and since Tamirandalia already had one), she gave it to Othir for Serifol, to enhance the animal's already keen nocturnal eyesight. Finally, Sinta was glad to let Valdira have the assassin's remarkable cloak, for the idea of trying to use it to fly terrified her.

With this business accomplished, Sinta and Othir took affectionate leave of their hosts, mounted their horses, and set out for Talindor. Sinta was now in the mood to discuss the case. Specifically, she wanted to mine Othir's knowledge of the princely court, for it was much more extensive than her own. Although she had on occasion been obliged, in the course of her brief affair with Halifor, to attend court functions at the castle, she had never felt comfortable there, as the daughter of a common apothecary, notwithstanding her vague rapport with Chancellor Thennis (who, unbeknownst to her, was the son of a saddler). By contrast, as an exceedingly handsome knight of the realm, Sir Othir moved easily among its socially exalted inhabitants, deriving, as a connoisseur of human folly, no small amusement from their many foibles.

"You know the court," Sinta said. "Explain its workings to me simply, as though I were a small but reasonably intelligent child—like Haldor."

Othir considered for a moment. "Well, as of course you know, Sildoor is one of the smaller sovereignties within Ondiran, so its court is also one of the smaller ones. Which is not to say it isn't considerably larger than it has any need to be, serving as it does chiefly to flatter the vanity of the prince, while providing harmless employment for the mostly superfluous scions of the principality's noble houses."

Sinta smiled. She had known she could count on Othir to provide a cynical assessment.

"I tend to think of the court as being in fact three courts," Othir continued. "The first is Prince Folgar's assemblage of men of high rank; the second, Princess-Consort Mirelde's collection of well-born ladies-in-waiting. While the members of those two courts perform many servile functions for the prince and princess, that fact in no way obviates the need for what I like to think of as the third court, namely the army of ordinary servants, who answer to the prince's chamberlain. In addition, of course, there's a separate body of servants at the prince's country estate, and another at his hunting lodge, each operating under its own steward. Finally, the court always entertains a few stray diplomats—though Sildoor isn't important enough to attract many—along with various wellborn hangers-on, office-seekers, and good-for-nothings, such as myself."

Sinta chuckled. "It seems to me we should at least be able to acquit the servants of being behind Halifor's murder. None of them could afford anything like sixteen princely crowns to hire an assassin."

"True, but at the same time no one will know more about what's going on in all three courts than they will."

Sinta nodded. "That's fair enough. So, what else can you tell me?"

Othir stroked his meticulously shaven chin (for merely staying up all night had not been enough to deflect him from his daily grooming regimen). "The structure of the courts is rigidly hierarchical, but not in the same way as one finds among, say, soldiery. Each court has a strict schedule of precedence, ranking each member in order from top to bottom, but almost everyone answers directly to the person at the top, not to whoever else happens to be above them. By virtue of his position, Chancellor Thennis, for example, ranks immediately below the prince, but so far as I know the only person who reports to him directly is his clerk, Ghelnor. Given Thennis's prestige and influence, lesser courtiers would be unwise to cross him, but they still answer to the prince, not the chancellor." He paused. "In any event, these people are all intensely status-conscious. Nothing is more important to them than their position in the schedule of precedence, which dictates everything about their lives at court, down to where they sit at the banquet table. I can readily imagine someone killing Lord Alfron over a petty rivalry, or from a hope of opening up the ladder of advancement."

Arriving in a large village, they stopped to water the horses at a trough fed by the fountain in the public square. Sinta got off to adjust her saddle. "So, tell me what you know about Lord Alfron," she said.

Othir offered Serifol a parsnip from his saddlebags. "Son of the late Baron of Coridan; younger brother of the current one; in his mid-forties, so about the same age as the prince, with whom he was close, apparently going back to childhood; one of two Gentlemen of the Chamber and holder of several rich sinecures; not bad looking for his age; a serial adulterer, unhappily married to Hrinde, who is one of the princess-consort's ladies-in-waiting and a pretty fierce creature in her own right. Frankly, Alfron reminded me of a particularly feather-brained gamecock, always strutting around in search of pretty pullets."

"Who do you suppose would have benefited from his death?"

Othir thought for a moment. "Well, Hrinde won't be shedding any tears, but I don't think she's likely to benefit financially. So far as I know, he wasn't a man of property. Any money will go to his worthless son, Frildar, but Alfron enjoyed living beyond his income, to the extent that he could, so I don't suppose Frildar's inheritance will amount to much, if anything at all. The sinecures revert to the crown, of course, and both the current baron and his son would have to die before Frildar would be in line for the barony." He picked a samara out of Serifol's mane. "Of course, Sir Thigtonil has benefited by taking Alfron's place as one of the Gentlemen of the Chamber, but he wasn't the only one who would have had his hopes of getting it."

"Who else would?"

"I'd have put my money on Lord Anthilor, the Baron of Toth's younger son. As Master of the Hounds, he's in charge of the prince's kennels, at least in theory. He's an incompetent fool, but the prince likes him."

"And Sir Thigtonil?"

"I was a little surprised to hear that he received the appointment. He's good-looking, ambitious, and clever—not the sort of person the prince usually keeps close—but he knows how to dissemble and ingratiate himself to those above him, so I suppose that explains it. Until now, he was Master of the Horse, which meant he supervised all the grooms and farriers, who actually look after the animals. The prince keeps a fine stable, and my impression is that Thigtonil was doing a good job there, which can't have hurt."

They remounted and continued on their way. Sinta normally enjoyed the scenery in this part of the valley, but today she had other concerns. "Just how desirable is being a Gentleman of the Chamber, anyway?"

Othir thought for a moment. "He attends the prince directly, by setting out his clothes and helping him dress—all that sort of thing. So, it's a position of great trust and influence. Of course, it's less important in this court than in many others, since Sildoor is so small, and its prince leaves most important matters to his chancellor, but I'm sure there are people who would kill to get the position all the same." He paused before adding, "Or to get it for their son."

Sinta looked at him sharply. "You suspect the Baron of Toth?"

Othir shook his head. "I don't know enough about him to say. Or about his wife. They don't spend as much time at court as some of the others. I gather they're too busy squeezing every last penny out of the peasants on their estate."

Sinta frowned. "So we have Alfron's wife, Hrinde, who hated him but doesn't stand to gain monetarily from his death; their son, Frildar, who doesn't stand to gain, either, but could, I suppose, have some unknown grievance against his father; Thigtonil, who succeeded Alfron as Gentleman of the Chamber; Anthilor, who also would have hoped to get the appointment—but, no, I met him once, and he struck me as too stupid to successfully poison anyone (other than perhaps himself, by accident); and finally the Baron of Toth and his wife, who may have hoped to engineer their son's preferment."

Othir nodded. "That about sums it up."

Sinta sighed. "What about Alfron's romantic entanglements. Do you know anything about those?"

Othir grinned. "Only a fraction of what there is to know, judging from that hamper we found. It's no great secret, however, that he recently dumped Lady Tisvena, the youngest child of the Baron of Ferigan, in favor of Esmilinde, the wife of Sir Topassin, Keeper of the Princely Seal. I believe Tisvena was pretty unhappy about it, and I can't imagine Sir Topassin was any too pleased, either."

Sinta rolled her eyes. "So, we add both of them to our list of suspects. There will also be people with older grievances of this sort, of course, but they seem less likely. I mean, why wait until now?"

❦

The two reached home in time for a late—and rather haphazard—supper. The cook had taken advantage of Sinta's absence to go visit her sister in a nearby village, so they warmed up some leftover vegetable stew made by the apothecary's wife, cut some slices of day-old bread, and divided an overripe plum, while leaving untouched some rather worrisome tripe. "Tomorrow," Sinta decided, "we'll report our progress—such as it is—to Chancellor Thennis and start interviewing potential witnesses."

"Do you suppose we could take our meals at the castle?" asked Othir, sniffing the watery stew with skepticism. "At least until Ferga gets back?"

8

Despite his common birth, Thennis rose to power in the Principality of Sildoor through a combination of ability, determination, and luck. Trained as a lawyer, he began his career as an assistant to Chancellor Volsin, who—lacking noteworthy talents of his own—rapidly became dependent on him. After a short stint as chief justice for the city of Talindor, Thennis was appointed chancellor by Prince Nohrinth II at the age of forty-six, and he held the position until his death thirty-two years later, during the reign of Prince Folgar I. He was considered a moderate in his political opinions and a pragmatist in his approach to governance.

—*Who Was Who in Medieval Ondiran*

"So, you let the assassin go?" Chancellor Thennis sounded neither pleased nor impressed.

Sinta and Othir had returned to the castle the next morning after an unsatisfying breakfast. "She didn't give us much choice," Sinta countered, "and we had no hard evidence against her—just my testimony regarding what I saw by the use of magic."

"Hmm." This point seemed to weigh with him. The intrusion of magic always complicated the adjudication of legal matters. "And now you are ready to start interviewing witnesses here at the castle?"

Sinta confirmed that they were. "We would like to begin with the kitchen and wait staff. Both to rule out any complicity and to see if we can determine exactly when the poison was introduced into the prince's food."

Thennis nodded approvingly. "That is acceptable. I'm afraid the prince does not wish for anyone of gentle birth to be subjected to the inconvenience and embarrassment of interrogation, unless there is substantial evidence inculpating them—" (his voice took on a subtly acerbic intonation that reminded Sinta of Othir) "—but the servants, of course, exist to be inconvenienced and embarrassed." He smiled. "Ghelnor will coordinate with the chamberlain to bring whomever you need up here to the chancellory. We have a suitably private room we can place at your disposal."

⚜

Some twenty minutes later, Ghelnor ushered in Shingach, the chief cook—or chef, as he preferred to call himself. A large man in his late forties, with a red face, bulging eyes, and close-cropped hair, he cut a rather alarming figure. Indeed, according to Ghelnor, he had once hurled a cleaver at a kitchen menial for preparing the wrong sauce to go with the asparagus.

"Why haff I been called here, heh?" he demanded with a thick Esdiric accent. The Esdir were not popular in Ondiran, but they had a reputation for being good cooks, and Sinta knew from her own—all too infrequent—experience dining at the castle that the prince was lucky to have him.

She cast a charm spell, but not her usual one. Although trained primarily in sorcery, Sinta was also highly conversant with wizardry (one of the other four major magical traditions of the known world), for Valdira had taken an ecumenical approach to her apprentice's magical education. This particular wizarding charm was notable for leaving the target with some convenient short-term memory loss. Although Sinta generally disapproved of the spell, which unscrupulous wizards were notorious for using to have their way with attractive members of the opposite (or indeed the same) sex, she considered its use here fully justified to preserve the secrecy of her investigation.

The cook's entire demeanor changed from that of a snarling mastiff to that of an ebullient puppy dog. "Wot can I do for you, miss?" he asked eagerly.

Sinta decided to conduct the interview in Esdiric. It was far from her best language, so she was pleased to have a chance to practice. Besides, Othir spoke it much better than she did, and she could rely on him to correct her or clarify any confusing points. She began, as she intended to begin all these interviews, with a simple admonition to tell the truth and omit nothing.

"Yes, of course!" Shingach exclaimed. "Why would I lie to such a charming lady, who speaks Esdiric so nicely?"

Sinta followed up with the two questions she would ask at every interview: did he administer the poison; if not, did he know who did?

Shingach answered both in the negative and looked hurt that she could suspect him of such villainy.

Might the poison have been introduced into the ingredients, prior to preparation?

Shingach did not see how that would have been possible. He had prepared seven pork tenderloins, which he had studded with garlic and roasted in a hot oven before introducing them to a sinfully rich cream sauce and garnishing them with fresh basil. (At this juncture, Sinta's mouth began to water, and Othir's face took on a dreamy expression.) Only when the tenderloins were finished did he choose the best of the seven to serve the prince. Since the court sorcerer's tests had established, had they not, that only the prince's tenderloin was poisoned, the fault surely could not have been in the previously indistinguishable ingredients.

Sinta asked exactly what happened after he chose the prince's tenderloin, prompting Shingach to explain that his assistant, Bervil, had laid the long slab of meat artistically upon an ornate silver platter and added generous helpings of buttered parsnips, carrots, and mushrooms. Shingach himself had then applied the cream sauce and fresh basil before shouting for the server Tarilor to carry the platter to the banquet hall.

Bervil was the next witness. A nervous young man with short hair and beady eyes, he confirmed Shingach's account without adding anything of note of his own, beyond warning that the chief cook, though brilliant, was nothing short of a fiend in human form.

Tarilor the server was a decidedly good-looking boy of sixteen. He had taken the platter from Shingach and hurried from the kitchen down the connecting corridor to the banquet hall, where he handed it to Lord Alfron. He had then returned immediately to the kitchen.

Sinta asked whether he had met anyone in the corridor.

The boy scratched his head. "I don't see how I could've. I remember leaving the kitchen, and I remember going into the banquet hall. I don't really remember going down the corridor somehow, apart from thinking how good the roast pork smelled, but if anybody'd been there, I'd have to remember *that,* wouldn't I?"

"You don't normally encounter other people in the corridor?"

"Just the other servers. On my way back, for instance, I met them bringing the other six platters of pork."

"But you didn't see any servers on your way to the banquet hall?"

"Oh, no. I wouldn't have, would I—they were all still in the kitchen then. The prince's pork tenderloin was the first dish of the main course to be taken in, you see. We'd already finished bussing the dirty dishes from the soup course."

Sinta thought for a moment. "Whom do you remember seeing in the banquet hall?"

Tarilor looked bemused. "I don't rightly know. Their Serene Highnesses, of course, and Lord Alfron, and, er, Pavia and Rovina. I wasn't really paying attention."

"Who are Pavia and Rovina?"

The boy blushed. Evidently he *had* been paying attention to *them.* "Two of the parlor maids. They look after the banquet hall."

"And you really don't remember anyone else?"

Tarilor closed his eyes, trying to picture the scene. "Lord Anthilor was telling some sort of joke, I think. Nobody seemed to think it was funny."

⚜

Interviewing the rest of the kitchen staff and servers took up the time remaining before lunch without adding anything of substance to the information Sinta had already gathered. Several of the servants confirmed that Shingach was an abominable person to work under. Indeed, one of the kitchen maids expressed the view that the chief cook should be put down like a dog.

Ghelnor then brought up an entire roast duck and several helpings of braised cabbage to share with Sinta and Othir, along with more modest fare for Chancellor Thennis, whose digestion was no longer what it once had been. Sinta cast a wizarding spell to neutralize poison, just in case.

"So, have you made any progress?" the chancellor wanted to know.

Sinta accepted her portion from Ghelnor and sat down. "After a fashion, Your Excellency," she replied. "It looks increasingly as though the poisoner used magic. I told you earlier that most fast-acting poisons are magical in nature. Now, we find that the server Tarilor has no memory of carrying the prince's dinner down the corridor connecting the kitchen with the banquet hall—the only place, as a practical matter, where someone could have added the poison to it. That suggests that the poisoner tampered with his memory."

Thennis looked grave. "I'm sorry to hear that. At least so far as I know, Halifor was the only one at court who had mystical powers, so the use of magic suggests the involvement of an outside agent. Of course, that could have been at the behest of someone at court—and Lord Alfron's death has definitely fanned existing factional rivalries—but I regret to say that the introduction of magic increases the likelihood of a broader plot. Therefore members of the diplomatic corps are in no way above suspicion. Keep that possibility in mind as you proceed."

❦

Now that Sinta was reasonably certain she had identified the scene of the crime, she asked Ghelnor to take her and Othir to the connecting corridor after lunch. As she suspected, it extended well beyond the passage between the kitchen and the banquet hall, so the poisoner could have come and gone without being observed from either of those places. Though pessimistic of her chances of success so long after the incident in question, she cast the "Speaking Stones" spell, which confirmed her deduction that Tarilor had briefly encountered someone in the corridor, but the passage of time had degraded the sensory traces retained by the stone walls and floor to such an extent that she could not even tell if it had been a man or a woman.

❦

To save time, Sinta decided to interview Pavia and Rovina together. The parlor maids giggled and made eyes at Othir, until Sinta charmed them and told them to behave themselves. She got the impression that Rovina had been charmed before, because the girl seemed to recognize what was happening and struggled briefly against the spell before succumbing to its power.

Although the two maids clearly regarded looking extremely pretty as their primary job, with the fetching of whatever might be needed in the banquet hall coming a distant second, they turned out to be close observers of events, who remembered in gossipy detail what they had witnessed on the "ever so exciting" day Lord Alfron died.

Between them they thus provided a vivid account of the meal, beginning with the gradual arrival of the twenty-odd guests, followed by the prince and the princess-consort. (The heir to the throne and his younger sister were not yet considered old enough to eat with the grown-ups, while the two older sisters were already married and no longer lived in Sildoor.) The girls related with relish a dramatic spat that had occurred between the "handsome" Baron of Toth and his "formidable" wife during the soup course, when she slapped him, called him a filthy pig, and stormed out of the banquet hall. They alluded to several off-color jokes told by "that oaf" Lord Anthilor, to the embarrassment of his "fussy" wife, Luria, while everyone waited for the main course. They giggled and blushed while describing Tarilor's arrival with the prince's meal (evidently, Sinta concluded, the attraction there was not all on one side). "He had a smudge of gravy on his forehead!" added Rovina, prompting a renewed gale of giggles from both girls. The boy had handed off the platter to "poor" Lord Alfron, who set it down before the prince and cut several slices of pork, one of which he sampled himself, along with a carrot, a parsnip, and two mushrooms. He then had just enough time to place the slices on the prince's plate, along with generous quantities of vegetables and fungi, before crying out in pain and falling violently to the floor, where he convulsed for a few seconds, then twitched, and then lay still. Both girls had screamed, as had the princess and a number of the other ladies present, while several of the gentlemen had risen from their seats, either to try to help Lord Alfron or to do some pointless shouting in the hope, as Rovina put it, of giving everyone the impression that they were men of action, who could take charge in a crisis. The other servers arrived almost immediately with the remaining trays of pork tenderloin, only to retreat in bumbling confusion back into the corridor. The agitated prince exited hastily with his bodyguard, the "dreamy" Sir Thanifor, followed by the distraught princess and her dearest friend among the ladies-in-waiting, the "sheep-faced" Lady Mara. Utter confusion reigned for several more minutes until someone had the presence of mind to summon Chancellor Thennis, who quickly restored order and sent Pavia to the kitchen to convey his strict instructions that none of the food prepared for the meal be thrown away, as there would have to be a thorough investigation.

Sinta took careful notes of all of this information, omitting only some of the more gratuitous adjectives. She then questioned the two girls closely to find out who had been present at the meal. Rovina's memory was particularly good, and Sinta was able to draw up a substantial list of people who could not have actually administered the poison, even if they might remain under suspicion of having arranged the killing. Lord Alfron's fellow Gentleman of the Chamber, the "dozy" Lord Fentimor, had thus been present, even though it was Lord Alfron's day to be taster. The victim's "boorish" son, Frildar, was already slightly drunk as the meal began, but his father's death appeared to shock him into something approaching sobriety. Lord Alfron's most recent conquest, the "pretty" but "stuck-up" Esmilinde, flirted "shamelessly" with him throughout the soup course but broke down upon his death and refused to be comforted.

Sinta probed specifically regarding her remaining preliminary suspects. Both girls were certain that Esmilinde's husband, Sir Topassin, had not been in attendance. Nor had Lord Alfron's recently abandoned lover, Lady Tisvena. The victim's estranged wife, "that old battleaxe" Lady Hrinde, was also absent, as was Lord Alfron's soon-to-be successor, the "handsome" but "handsy" Sir Thigtonil.

Mindful of the chancellor's admonition about possible foreign involvement, Sinta asked about the five diplomatic envoys credentialed to Sildoor (the principality not being important enough to exchange ambassadors). Only the one from Fendoran had been present. His colleagues from Ool, Menfir, Mar-Faldot, and Mar-Tigret had not, but that was apparently typical. "We don't see the diplomats here very often," explained Rovina. "Which is a pity," sighed Pavia. "I'd give myself to that envoy from Mar-Tigret in a heartbeat!"

⚜

Sinta took her list of guests to Chancellor Thennis, who was able to confirm most of the names from his own memory of the day. He also added one, that of an unobtrusive middle-aged functionary the parlor maids had overlooked. "I suppose he may turn out to be a criminal mastermind," Thennis noted drily, "but the poor fellow looked as though he had never so much as seen a dead body before."

Sinta decided to focus next on those servants who had direct connections to the victim and his family, while Othir proposed that he seek another perspective on events in the banquet hall from the prince's bodyguard, Sir Thanifor, whom he knew tolerably well (and, Sinta suspected, would like to know far better). Chancellor Thennis decided that a friendly chat would not violate the prince's edict regarding interrogations, so off Othir went.

Sinta began with Togir, Lord Alfron's valet. He was an unprepossessing little man in his early twenties, with greasy hair and a cringing manner. Sinta disliked him on sight. She quickly established that he had been in Alfron's service for only six months and that he did not consider the man a particularly good master, though he greatly admired his success with women. (Sinta could not imagine that Togir himself had much luck in that department.)

"Oh, the master knew how to hook an' gaff 'em!" he cackled.

Sinta felt that anyone who compared women to fish deserved a celibate life, but she refrained from saying so.

Instead, she asked for names, which Togir was happy to provide, and probably would have been even had he not been under a charm spell. In addition to Esmilinde and Lady Tisvena, Alfron's recent conquests included Lady Floria (the youngest daughter of the Baron of Ninthan) and Drinna (the wife of Sir Rildan, the prince's herald). Additionally, he had prevailed once or twice upon Lady Floria's sixteen-year-old maid, Sia, an indiscretion that had brought his affair with the girl's mistress to an abrupt conclusion, when the lady caught them together *in flagrante.*

Sinta compared these names with her list of attendees at the banquet hall. Lady Floria had been there, as a recent accession to the ranks of the princess's ladies-in-waiting. Sir Rildan the herald had been there, too, but without his wife. Sinta sighed. More suspects, and Togir's knowledge went back only six months. She looked up from her notes at the unctuous valet, who was bowing and scraping out of pure force of habit. Had anyone made any threats against Lord Alfron recently?

Togir laughed. "Threats? Why, just a week before, it must've been, that Sir Topassin told my master, if he didn't keep his ruttin' hands off Sir Topassin's wife, he'd gut 'im like a river trout!"

Sinta raised an eyebrow. "And what did Lord Alfron say to that?"

Togir grinned. "Why, he just laughed in his face and said, 'If you can't satisfy that pretty little bitch of yours when she's in heat, you should make way for someone who can!'"

Sinta made a note of this alleged exchange and marked it heavily in the margin.

⸙

Othir found Sir Thanifor exercising in one of the castle's inner courtyards and suggested some friendly swordplay. "Sinta and I are just back from Tserenets, where I finally got my hands on an enchanted blade," he explained, "but I still need to teach it who's boss." He showed Thanifor the gleaming weapon, a superbly crafted broadsword, well-balanced, with a fine leather grip and a pommel in the shape of a badger's head.

Thanifor expressed his admiration. His own magic sword, though highly effective, was less artistically made.

They began to fight, Othir somewhat clumsily. "The wretched thing really has its heart set on getting me killed!" he complained.

Thanifor parried an awkward thrust. "Trust me, it'll take awhile for it to come around. Mine had it in for me for weeks, but now it's like an extension of my own body."

Othir looked for an opening. "Say, I really missed all the excitement, didn't I? It's not every day someone tries to poison the prince." He feinted left.

Thanifor saw through the feint and riposted, scoring a hit on Othir's armor. "Thank goodness for that! My job's hard enough without bringing poisoners into the picture."

Othir fumbled and dropped his weapon. "Damn it! I've had enough of this blade's nonsense for now. Tell me what happened. I haven't had a chance yet to hear the whole story."

Thanifor twirled his sword and went over to get a drink of water from the cistern in the middle of the courtyard. "It was quite a day!"

His account tallied with that of the two parlor maids, though he took a more charitable view of Lord Anthilor's unfunny jokes, which he saw as a clumsy attempt by the man to cover his mortification at his parents' public scene. "Anthilor's a fool," Thanifor acknowledged, "but he has feelings, just like the rest of us."

Thanifor also recalled that the prince's falconer, Sir Rodor, had reacted to Alfron's collapse by crossing his arms and smiling. "But then, Alfron knocked up Rodor's daughter a couple of years back, so I suppose he had every right to be pleased."

Othir expressed surprise that he had not caught wind of such a juicy scandal at the time.

"Oh, they covered it up, all right. The girl was sent away to a Zoorist convent in Mar-Rendet, and the baby went to some childless couple, when it came. I remember Rodor telling me he'd feed Alfron's bollocks to the prince's falcons one day. But I guess watching him drop dead from poison must've scratched the same itch."

Sinta was waiting for Ghelnor to bring her next interview subject to the chancellory, when Othir returned. She listened to Thanifor's revelations with interest and told Othir the substance of Togir's. "Our list of suspects keeps growing," she noted. "It would be nice if we'd find some actual evidence that pared it back down."

Their conversation was cut short, however, by the arrival of Dherghita, lady's maid to Lord Alfron's widow. A tiny, birdlike creature of about fifty with steel-gray hair pulled into a tight bun, she was originally from the northern Duchy of Trusilor and spoke the Ondiric dialect prevalent there with considerable verve.

"Good heavens, no!" she exclaimed, upon being asked if she had poisoned Alfron. "Bless you, child, whatever makes you think I could do such a thing? Mind you, if ever a man deserved to be poisoned, his lordship was that man. Half-tomcat, he must have been, the way he cheated on my poor mistress!"

Sinta suggested that Lady Hrinde thus had a motive to kill him.

"Motive?" Dherghita chirped. "Of course she had a motive! But then, who didn't?"

Further questions revealed that Lady Hrinde had in fact often expressed the hope of seeing her husband dead in a ditch someday, though Dherghita had never heard her say anything suggesting she intended to make it happen. Dherghita did not know where her mistress had been at the time of the murder, but she was certain the woman had not the slightest acquaintance with either poisons or magic. "Her ladyship wouldn't know how to boil an egg," she told them, "let alone brew a deadly poison."

The last interview of the day was with Nintor, valet to the victim's son, Frildar. An unexceptional looking man of about thirty-five, he dressed carefully and spoke precisely, enunciating his words as though he were declaiming a literarily significant but tedious epic poem. Had Sinta had the opportunity to read the Ondiric comedies of manners written several centuries later, she would have recognized him as the quintessential elite manservant.

When Nintor denied poisoning Lord Alfron, his face displayed the same bland indifference with which he would have denied that his master was at home to visitors, and Sinta began to wonder if her charm spell had been effective. She asked about Frildar.

"I have no cause to suspect the young master," he replied, perfectly achieving the affect of a stuffed owl.

As Sinta pursued her line of questioning, however, she concluded that her spell had in fact worked. Constrained to tell the truth, Nintor had a good deal to say about his employer that she sensed he would normally have considered it his duty to conceal. The young master might not be a murderer, but he had no self-respect and less self-discipline. His father had arranged a nominal position for him, as Keeper of the Talindor Wells and Fountains, but what little money it afforded he spent on wine and paid female companionship. (Sinta expressed alarm that such a wastrel might be responsible for the city's water supply, but Nintor assured her it was a sinecure, and some poorly paid municipal official attended to any actual work.) Having sided with his father against his mother over the failure of their marriage, Frildar was a bitter disappointment to Lady Hrinde, who resolutely refused to finance his dissolute lifestyle. No, Frildar had no expectation of inheritance from either parent. Had he quarreled recently with his father? No, at least, not any more than usual. "Indeed," Nintor concluded, "encountering him shortly after Lord Alfron's death, I thought the young master seemed genuinely distressed—but I suppose he may simply have been hung over."

9

Medieval Ondiric funerary rites varied significantly, depending upon the faith of the departed. Asardians and Cantiferians required burial, Hrintists and Zoorists cremation. Cantiferianism advocated a long and festive celebration of the deceased's life, while Hrintism dictated rapid disposal of the body with a minimum of fuss. Asardian services invariably featured hymns of great musical complexity and beauty, whereas Zoorists preferred rhythmic chanting in which the entire congregation could take part.

—*Everyday Life in Medieval Ondiran*

After a meager supper at the apothecary's shop, Sinta and Othir returned to the castle for Halifor's funeral. Ghelnor had undertaken the arrangements, for the court sorcerer's parents lived far to the northwest in the Margravate of Voral. Word of his death was unlikely to reach them for some time.

Halifor had been raised in the Lorventinian faith, an obscure northern religion he had once described to Sinta as "irretrievably gloomy." The court had no Lorventinian minister in residence to officiate, but the resourceful Ghelnor managed to find an itinerant preacher of that persuasion in Mar-Beran. Simply dressed, all in black, this man was quite ancient, with wispy white hair, a scraggly beard, and rheumy eyes, but he retained a strong speaking voice, as well as a hectoring manner not uncommon among the Ondiric clergy, especially those of the older generation.

The court chapel was available to all religious denominations upon application to the prince's chamberlain, and the cloying smell of incense still hung in the air from a Cantiferian name-giving ceremony earlier in the day. The vaulted chamber was a rare survival of the spare and elegant early Rendiric style, but it was now dark, lit only by a pair of wax tapers the preacher carried with him. Aided by their magic rings, however, Sinta and Othir could see that the service was poorly attended. As a commoner, Halifor was evidently beneath the notice of most members of the court. To be sure, Chancellor Thennis was there, looking pensive. Sir Rildan the herald, Sir Rodor the falconer, and Sir Topassin, Keeper of the Princely Seal, had also seen fit to attend, along with two other men of quality, whom Sinta did not recognize. Though Halifor had retained no valet, the maid who cleaned for him was sitting at the back, together with a handful of townspeople the sorcerer had befriended, including the local alchemist, a man named Dvortin.

The preacher began by expounding that funerals should always be held at night, since death represented the spirit's entry into "the blessed oblivion of eternal darkness." He then delivered a dreary sermon on the subject of sin. (To no one's surprise, he came out against it.) While Halifor's murder seemed to Sinta the obvious jumping off point for this topic, the preacher preferred to emphasize lust, gluttony, and drunkenness. In the process he managed to suggest that his listeners were desperate libertines, who—notwithstanding the solemnity of the occasion—were surely thinking about fornication at that very moment.

"Well, if we weren't doing so before," Othir whispered to Sinta, "I'm sure most of us are now!"

Long passages from the Lorventinian liturgy followed, all in the ancient Gantelic tongue. Sinta, who had studied Gantelic as an apprentice, recognized most of the words, but her understanding foundered on their opaque theological content. Othir, who knew no Gantelic at all, now definitely began thinking about fornication, which seemed to him a far better way of spending his time than listening to the babbling of an elderly religious fanatic.

The preacher closed with a brief eulogy—brief by necessity, since he had not known Halifor and knew nothing about him. He therefore spoke in platitudes, concluding sourly that the dead man's passing should be regarded with equanimity rather than sorrow, for death represented a release from the trials and tribulations of this mortal coil. "We are, all of us, ultimately food for worms," he noted, seeming to brighten slightly at the prospect, "so let us now reflect on that as we pass outside into the fitting blackness of night and commit this man's body to the ground."

"I'm sorry, Sinta," Ghelnor said, embarrassed, as the preacher tottered out of the chapel with his tapers, leaving it in darkness. "I didn't realize how awful that would be."

Sinta shook her head. "It *was* awful," she conceded, casting a dim light with her wand, "but it was so *truly* awful I think Halifor would have enjoyed it." She sighed reminiscently and wiped away a tear. "He had a talent for finding humor in the most unlikely places."

"He was a good fellow," said Sir Rodor. "He knew who he was—not like some of the folk around here, who only think they do."

"He was a good neighbor," agreed Sir Rildan, whose workshop lay beneath Halifor's own, "even if I did sometimes worry that he might accidentally blast our tower off its foundation."

Othir took his employer's arm as they traversed two small courtyards to reach the castle's modest cemetery. A widespread Ondiric superstition against bringing a corpse into a place of worship meant that Halifor's body had been waiting patiently in the graveyard during the service. The two gravediggers Ghelnor had hired for the job, upon seeing the mourners approach, cut short the game of knucklebones they had been playing on the lid of the coffin and took up a position a few yards away, holding up their shovels like halberds and trying to look respectful, albeit with scant success.

Abundant moonlight bathed the cemetery in silver, as the preacher recited a Gantelic prayer, in which the words for "oblivion" and "blessed darkness" featured prominently. Able to see his congregation better here than in the chapel, he glared at Sinta and at Halifor's former maid, for northern custom banned women from attending funerals (apart from their own, of course).

Sinta fought the urge to laugh at this appalling person, but soon she was struggling to hold back tears instead, as the two gravediggers lowered the simple wooden box holding all that was mortal of her friend and former lover into the pitch-black void they had excavated in the earth. Then, as heavy clods of soil fell from their shovels and resounded with hollow thuds upon the coffin lid, the dam broke and Sinta wept.

10

Although the baron with his barony constituted the fundamental building block of the former feudal system in Ondiran, the theoretically ascending hierarchy of higher nobility—the burgraves, counts, margraves, dukes, princes, grand dukes, and kings—was beset in practice by a gross inconsistency, for a count possessed of thirty baronies exercised vastly more power in imperial affairs than a grand duke who might have only two. Indeed, the emperor himself was the ultimate symbol of this power imbalance, for his writ rarely ran beyond the imperial city of Vildenon.

—*The Phantom Empire: A Historical Geography of Ondiran*

Sinta awoke the next morning determined to make progress in the investigation. "Let's see if we can't turn up some hard evidence before we do any more interviews today," she suggested over breakfast. (Ferga the cook had returned, so the meal was filling, not to say heavy.) "Perhaps investigating the poison will lead us to the poisoner." Sinta therefore assigned Othir to visit the major vendors of fruit in the city to see if anyone had been buying undue quantities of peaches, apricots, plums, or cherries, all of which happened to be in season. She herself would visit Dvortin the alchemist in search of information regarding magical poisons.

Talindor was built into the steeply rising left bank of the Vassata, and the alchemist's shop stood at the top of the hill, an energetic climb from the town square. Once she got there, Sinta paused, as she usually did, to catch her breath and admire the view of the prince's castle, located on the even taller hill rising from the right bank.

"Greetings, Master Dvortin," she said upon entering the shop, which smelled—as it usually did—as though the alchemist had been burning something better left in its natural state. "Has anyone been in lately to buy ingredients for fast-acting magical poisons?"

A grizzled man of about fifty, though he looked older, the alchemist considered Sinta's question for a moment. In the three years since the sorceress had returned to Talindor, he had become accustomed to her coming to him with odd queries. As she sometimes also bought things, he chose to tolerate it. "Well, someone came in yesterday asking for yarrow, which is one of several ingredients needed to produce the sorcerer's poison known as the 'Headsman's Axe,' but I don't stock it, so I referred him to your shop."

Sinta shook her head. "Earlier than that. I'm looking into the poisoning of Lord Alfron twelve days ago."

Dvortin frowned. "Someone bought a little saltpeter around that time, but it's only one of about eight ingredients for the wizard's poison 'Hell's Bells,' and he didn't ask for any of the others. Besides, saltpeter has other perfectly legitimate uses."

Seeing that this line of inquiry was not getting her anywhere, Sinta asked the alchemist instead for general information about fast-acting magical poisons. It was one of the few magical subjects concerning which Valdira had failed to instruct her in detail.

Dvortin proved happy to discourse at length on the topic, revealing that the poison known as the "Sweet Kiss Goodnight" involved magically hastening the naturally occurring toxin in foxgloves, while "Falir's Death Drops" were manufactured from the perfectly harmless primrose flower, and "Borva's Royal Remedy" required draining the blood from an ox-tongue and combining it with three different chemical compounds and two rare herbs. "It's too bad you can't ask Halifor," he concluded. "Collecting recipes for magical poisons was sort of a hobby of his."

Sinta started. This was news to her!

"Oh, I don't think he ever actually used them. But he was determined to get to the bottom of the underlying magical principles." Dvortin scratched his head with his left hand, which was missing two fingers. "Incidentally, I've heard that witches have a simple spell to turn food poisonous without their having to go to the trouble of brewing something, and then sneaking it into someone's supper, all the while worrying about how to disguise the taste of the stuff. But you know how it is with witches. Secretive critters. Who knows whether it's true or not."

Sinta looked at the alchemist with interest. Learning more about witchcraft was a long-standing ambition of hers. Of the five major systems of magic, it was the one about which outsiders knew the least, for its cagey practitioners guarded their arcana jealously. "Thank you, Master Dvortin," she said, after musing on the matter for a moment. "All of this has been most helpful."

⚜

Sinta reached the castle before Othir and therefore began her interviews without him. As Sir Topassin had recently threatened Lord Alfron's life, she decided to begin with his valet together with his wife's maid. Since they would both be under a charm spell, she could see no need to speak with them separately. Although Sinta had met Sir Topassin, she had not seen enough of him to form an opinion of his character. She knew that as Keeper of the Princely Seal he held a position of trust and responsibility.

Rovon, the valet, was an elderly man, stooped, hard of hearing, and nearly bald, while Talira, Esmilinde's maid-servant, was middle-aged, plump, and matronly. Both denied any knowledge of who had poisoned Lord Alfron.

"The master and Lord Alfron used to be such friends," Rovon recalled. "They grew up together along with the prince. But they drifted apart, you know, later in life, as they competed for position and influence with His Serene Highness. And then, of course, they fell out completely over the mistress." His face took on a censorious expression. "The master should never have married someone so much younger than himself. But she really set her cap at him, that girl did. Determined, she was, to marry her way into a place at court. And she is a pretty little thing!"

Talira snorted. "Not real gentry, that girl. Daughter of the daughter of some upstart knight or other, but she treats you like she's the Queen of Quintiran and you're just pond scum." (Quintiran was the mythic kingdom in which most Ondiric fairytales were set.) "Poor Sir Topassin should have known better, but then he wasn't exactly thinking with his brain when he married her." Delicacy apparently forbade mention of the organ with which he had been thinking instead.

Sinta had no reason to suspect Esmilinde, so she sought to redirect the discussion into a more promising channel.

Rovon confirmed that Sir Topassin had threatened more than once to kill Lord Alfron but denied that his master would ever consider using poison. "He was a decent swordsman as a lad. No, if he meant to kill him, he would have used a blade and done it in a fair duel."

Talira had heard Sir Topassin tell Esmilinde that he would kill Lord Alfron, but she had to agree with Rovon that he would not have done it with poison. Both servants admitted that they did not know where Sir Topassin had been at the time of the poisoning, but they denied that he knew anything about magic or had any connection with magicians, apart from his acquaintance with Halifor, the court sorcerer. No, the two were not friends, exactly, but they got along well enough—considering the sorcerer's low birth.

Servants, Sinta reflected, could be every bit as snooty as their masters.

At this point, Othir arrived, looking vaguely disgruntled. Sinta asked the two servants a few more questions but learned nothing more that she thought important. She sent them on their way and filled Othir in on what they had told her. As she did so, the alarming possibility occurred to her that Halifor himself could have poisoned

Lord Alfron, acting at Sir Topassin's behest. She explained what she had learned at the alchemist's.

To her relief, Othir found this theory unconvincing. "Well, you knew Halifor better than I did," he said, "but I can't imagine him poisoning anyone, not unless he had a strong motive of his own to commit murder." His voice took on a mischievous intonation. "He wasn't jealous of your grand passion with Alfron, was he?" (Sinta stifled an undignified giggle.) "Besides, who hired the assassin to kill Halifor, then? No one appears to have cared enough about Alfron to want to avenge his death. On the contrary, it seems that a lot of people would gladly have given the poisoner a slap on the back. And all of this assumes that someone figured out that Halifor was the killer in the first place, which seems unlikely. That just leaves Topassin, who would have known, of course. I suppose he might have had him killed to cover his tracks, but why would he need to? As the poisoner himself, Halifor would have been in no position to blackmail him."

Sinta was happy to let herself be dissuaded. "Tell me about your adventures among the fruit dealers," she suggested.

Othir grimaced. "I attended the premises of six such merchants, or fruiterers, as they are pleased to style themselves. None reported bulk sales any more suspicious than a hundredweight of ripe peaches to the weavers' guild for their annual—and no doubt orgiastic—gala two weeks ago. This is apart, of course, from the usual consignments of stone fruit—or drupe, as I am advised the technical term is—to the castle, care of Ghiron, who is responsible for all purchases of fresh produce for the court." (Sinta made a note of the name.) "In short, my mission was unsuccessful—indeed I would term it fruitless, had I not seized the opportunity to purchase some ripe cherries for our lunch." He produced a bulging cloth bag. "They are," he noted, extracting one and placing it in his mouth, "sweet and extremely succulent."

Sinta commended him on this admirable display of initiative and helped herself to a piece of the dark red, gem-like fruit.

⚜

The next suspect on Sinta's list was Sir Rodor, the falconer, who had made such unpleasant threats regarding the disposition of Lord Alfron's testicles. Sinta knew the man slightly and liked him. She had gone with him to the mews once to see the prince's hawks and falcons—beautiful creatures, she thought, though also alarming with their sharp beaks and unforgiving talons. Like Halifor, Sir Rodor had no valet, for he insisted that he had been perfectly capable of dressing himself since he was a small child, thank you very much. Fortunately, he did have a young assistant named Fovil, whom he was training to be a falconer himself one day.

The boy was about fifteen, with flowing black hair and an engaging smile. He had just started working at the mews when Lord Alfron had gotten Sir Rodor's daughter pregnant, so he remembered the matter well. "I've never seen Sir Rodor so angry," he admitted, "not even when I messed up and let a newly captured goshawk escape before we could train it." He shook his head. "I don't think he killed him, though. My master's a gentle man, really, beneath the bluster."

Othir asked about the day of the banquet. Having uncovered the lead regarding Sir Rodor in the first place, he was hoping it would prove to be the crux of their investigation.

Fovil considered the question for a moment. "Oh, he was definitely glad Lord Alfron snuffed it. He came home in quite a good mood. I just don't think he killed him."

Sinta asked about poisons and magic, and Fovil admitted that his master knew a fair amount about naturally occurring toxins, though he preferred to use traps to catch vermin, which he could then feed to the prince's birds without harming them. The boy doubted very much, however, that his master knew anything about magic or was acquainted with any magicians, "apart from Halifor—and you, of course, miss."

Sinta gave the boy some cherries and let him return to the mews. "I think we can discount Sir Rodor," she told Othir. "For one thing, if he had been behind the poisoning, surely he would have pretended to be shocked rather than pleased when it happened."

After lunch, Sinta asked to speak with the servants who attended upon Lord Anthilor and his wife, Luria. She remained convinced that Anthilor was too stupid to have conceived a plot to poison anyone, but Luria was an unknown quantity, who might perhaps have schemed to advance her husband's career by engineering a convenient vacancy close to the prince—with or without Anthilor's knowledge. Both had been present in the banquet hall, however, so they would have needed someone else to administer the poison—and presumably to prepare or procure it, as well.

Sinta was also ready to hear about something other than Lord Alfron's overactive love life.

Unsurprisingly, neither of the two servants confessed to poisoning the pork tenderloin. Figgin, Lord Anthilor's valet, laughed out loud at the very idea and laughed even harder at the suggestion that his master might have had anything to do with it. A large, jolly fellow in his mid-forties, he had no respect for Anthilor, whom he described as a "drooling halfwit." (By contrast, Anthilor's elder brother, Lord Caador, and sister, Lady Terinifulte, were both "as clever as can be.")

Firente, Luria's maid, was more circumspect, but she had to agree that Anthilor's intellect was less than impressive. A fresh-faced country girl, who had been in service for less than a year, she admitted to being afraid of her mistress, a hard woman from a merchant background, who had married above her station and hoped to rise still further. Firente had no reason to think Luria knew anything about poisons or magic, but she would not put anything past her. "When Lord Alfron died, she certainly made the case for appointing her husband in his place to anyone who would listen."

"And to lots of people who wouldn't!" interjected Figgin with a ringing laugh.

Othir inquired about Lord Anthilor's parents, the Baron of Toth and his wife.

Both servants went quiet for a moment.

"Grasping, they are," offered Figgin. "They make moneylenders look like fluffy kittens."

Firente acknowledged that she found the baroness even more perturbing than she did Luria.

"That old witch is another of these jumped-up commoners," said Figgin. "Hard as nails, she is, and twice as sharp!"

Sinta pricked up her ears at the word "witch," but Figgin assured her it was just an expression. "She was a great beauty once," he added, "and she's still quite a handsome lady, but you don't ever want to cross her."

With the departure of Figgin and Firente, Sinta asked Othir for information on Anthilor's siblings, Lord Caador and Lady Terinifulte. "This is the first I've heard of them," she noted. "Neither is on my list of people in the banquet hall, so from that point of view I suppose either one could be the poisoner."

Othir's face took on a wistful expression, which suggested to Sinta that the brother must be both good-looking and unavailable. "Caador serves as adjutant to the prince's captain of the guard," he said. "He's pretty much everything Anthilor isn't: strong, handsome, and clever." He sighed regretfully. "No, Caador's a good officer, and the men respect him. Strict but fair, when it comes to enforcing the captain's discipline. While I wouldn't think poison would be his weapon of choice, I suppose you never can tell." Othir reflected for a moment. "I've never met the sister," he continued. "She doesn't come to court. But they say she's beautiful. She really should be married by now, but apparently she's strong-minded and has the sense to be particular about who she'll be stuck with for the rest of her life."

Sinta decided they should speak with Caador's squire, a lad named Selnov. Although he was of gentle birth, Sinta promised Ghelnor that the boy would experience very little "inconvenience and embarrassment" from an interview that he would not even remember afterward, while Othir pointed out—speaking from personal experience—that the life of a squire consisted largely of inconvenience and embarrassment in any case.

Just thirteen, Selnov had been in Caador's service for only a few months, but he did not hesitate to endorse Othir's good opinion of his master. "He only punishes me when I really mess up," he explained, "and he doesn't misuse me the way some knights do their squires." He shuddered. "The things I hear about sometimes!"

When Sinta asked about Caador's whereabouts at the time of the poisoning, Selnov pleaded ignorance, for he had been busy polishing his master's best boots. He could not, however, credit the notion that Caador might have been involved in such a thing. "He's an honorable man, is his lordship, and there's nothing honorable about poisoning someone, is there."

"But mightn't he have felt a duty to help his brother?" Sinta asked.

Selnov looked astonished. "Lord Anthilor?" He considered the idea carefully. "Yes, I suppose he might. But I think he would have found some way other than murder."

Othir inquired about Caador's parents, the Baron and Baroness of Toth. What were they like?

Selnov replied, with evident relief, that he had not seen much of them in the short time he had been in his lordship's service. The baron, he acknowledged, could be very stern, while the baroness was downright frightening. "When I visited their estate at Toth for the first time, my master warned me to steer clear of her. 'Her ladyship believes in punishing boys who make mistakes,' he told me. 'Trust me—you don't want to make any!'"

Next up was Lady Tisvena's maid, Tirana. While they waited for her to arrive, Sinta asked Othir to refresh her memory. "I know Tisvena was Alfron's latest conquest but one. What else can you tell me about her?"

Othir finished off the last of the cherries. "Well, she's the youngest child of the Baron of Ferigan. The baron and his wife spend very little time in court, so I don't know much about them, except that they're filthy rich. His wife brought substantial properties in the County of Menfir to the marriage, and I believe he has an interest in one of the Fendoric tin mines, as well. Tisvena joined the court as a lady-in-waiting last year, when she came of age. I have the impression that she was pretty broken up when Alfron dropped her in favor of Esmilinde, though I can't imagine what the silly girl was expecting from the relationship, since Alfron was already married."

Ghelnor escorted Tirana into the room, and Sinta threw the wizarding charm spell on her. The woman denied any role in the poisoning, as well as any knowledge of who might have done it. An elderly woman, originally from western Ondiran, she had spent so many years in Talindor that her western accent had faded away to almost nothing. She obviously felt fiercely protective toward her naive young mistress, deeply regretted the girl's ill-judged affair, and hated Lord Alfron for "defiling" such a sweet, innocent child. "I hope the poison didn't just afflict his body," Tirana declared. "I hope it burned away his wicked soul." She bemoaned the lack of interest the girl's parents had shown in the whole matter. Having four sons, they evidently regarded Tisvena as surplus to requirements. None of the girl's brothers seemed to think much of her, either. No, Tisvena knew nothing about poisons, or magic, or magicians, or any of the other sad realities of life. The poor child lived in a romantic fairyland, which that cad Lord Alfron had brought crashing down around her. And yes, she knew exactly where Tisvena was at the time of the poisoning—in her bedchamber, crying her eyes out.

Sinta and Othir exchanged looks, pleased to be able to eliminate a suspect for once without adding several new ones in her place.

They were pleased to rule out the next two, as well, when the body servants for the prince's herald, Sir Rildan, and his wife, Drinna, both firmly attested that neither had any real motive. Rildan and Alfron had been friends, while Rildan and Drinna disliked one another. Rildan had therefore been indifferent to Drinna's affair with Alfron, as was she to his own current fling with the wife of one of the town councilors. Moreover, far from having been dumped by Alfron, Drinna had been the one to end their relationship in order to pursue a handsome squire half her age.

Consulting her notes, Sinta decided they had time for one last interview related to Lord Alfron's philandering before calling it a day. Ghelnor accordingly summoned Lady Floria's current maid, Talla, a homely young woman with bad skin and a sour expression. Evidently, Sinta thought, Lady Floria had drawn certain conclusions from having caught her previous, pretty maid, Sia, with Lord Alfron.

Talla had been with Lady Floria for ten months. She knew Sia had been expelled from the castle in disgrace, but nothing more about the foolish girl's fate. Lady Floria, now nineteen, was a similarly foolish creature, easy prey for Lord Alfron, of whom Talla had a low opinion. Admittedly, Floria had managed to conceal the affair from her parents, the Baron and Baroness of Ninthan, but that had not required a great deal of cleverness. So far as Talla could see, the baron and baroness were not very clever themselves. Aristocrats had no need to be clever, for they had the power to do what they wanted regardless.

How had Lady Floria reacted to Lord Alfron's death? She had been surprised, certainly, but she had returned from the banquet hall more interested in trying a new way of wearing her hair than she was in talking about the murder. No, Floria had put Lord Alfron behind her, where he belonged. Magic? Floria's knowledge of magic—or really any other practical subject—could, in Talla's view, easily be contained within a thimble. What the young flibbertigibbet needed was to find a sensible, if undiscriminating, husband to make all her decisions for her and generally keep her out of trouble.

Sinta dismissed the woman and began to think about supper. She had asked Ghelnor to arrange for her and Othir to take the meal in the banquet hall, so she would have a chance to observe at least some of the suspects for herself. It had been a long day, and she was looking forward to finding out what culinary delights Shingach had in store for them.

11

Take steaks of beef or venison and griddle them in fat until browned; then baste with a wine and vinegar sauce using powdered spices such as pepper, ginger, and cinnamon; garnish with fresh herbs and serve.

—*The Cookery of Esdiron, Explained*

The banquet hall was a long, high-ceilinged chamber that still retained the faint, lingering aroma of the day's delicious lunch. At the near end, above the main entrance, was a gallery from which minstrels sometimes performed, though on this occasion none were present. A banquet table made of a dark hardwood, probably walnut, with elaborate designs of pewter inlay, ran almost the full length of the room. It currently bore twenty-six expensive place settings, while five silver candelabra supplemented the light from three cut-glass chandeliers overhead, all fitted with the highest quality beeswax candles. Rich tapestries served to muffle the echo of voices off the walls, while thick carpets muted footfalls on the floor. The hall had reasonably good acoustics as a result, so Sinta could expect to overhear the other guests' conversations, even at a distance, so long as there were not too many underway at once. To be sure, given her severely deficient social status, she would be seated as far from the prince and princess as could be contrived. Othir, as a knight of the realm, would receive more favorable treatment.

The two investigators and their minder were among the last to reach the hall. As it would be a grave social miscue to arrive after Their Serene Highnesses, most courtiers took pains to come early, filling any extra time with idle chatter. Sir Rodor, the falconer, looking typically hale and ruddy, had thus already taken his seat near the unfashionable end of the table. "Mistress Sinta," he exclaimed, rising as Ghelnor guided her to her place, "it's good to see you here. Am I right in thinking you must be taking up poor Halifor's investigation?"

Sinta flushed, conscious that everyone had turned to look at her. "N-no, not at all!" she stammered. She was not a good liar. "No, I don't want to be murdered in the night!"

Ghelnor intervened quickly on her behalf. "Following the court sorcerer's unfortunate demise," he explained smoothly, "Mistress Sinta has been helping to protect the prince by using her magicks to eliminate any poison that might be present in his food and drink." Ghelnor's job sometimes required artful deviations from the narrow path of truth. "The chancellor felt it only right to spare her the heat of the kitchen on such a warm evening."

Sinta gave him a grateful smile for this graceful save, but she feared the damage had been done.

"My understanding," Othir added, "is that the chancellor has handed the investigation over to a *man,* as is right and proper." Thanks to the exigencies of his auntish upbringing, he too was practiced at the art of deception. He also enjoyed the occasional opportunity to tease Sinta.

"Well, that's good news," said a dissolute-looking fellow further up the table, who Sinta later realized was Lord Alfron's good-for-nothing son, Frildar. "We need the investigation done right!"

A redoubtable woman even further up the table (Frildar's estranged mother, Lady Hrinde) gave an indignant sniff, without making it clear whether her disapproval attached to her son on general principle, his apparent attitude toward the competence of women in particular, the desirability of a successful investigation into her husband's death, or possibly all three at once.

"Ah, well," said an unusually handsome young man near the head of the table, taking a mildly ironic tone, "let us hope this mysterious individual" (he looked directly at Sinta, who had the uncomfortable feeling he was not deceived) "will soon discover the culprit."

"Hear, hear, Lord Caador!" declared a comely young blonde woman a third of the way up the table, to the obvious irritation of her red-faced, fortyish husband, Sir Topassin. So, Sinta thought, this must be Esmilinde, Lord Alfron's final paramour.

The sorceress turned her attention instead, however, to the alleged Lord Caador, son and heir of the Baron of Toth. He was well worth looking at, with dark hair and eyes, chiseled features, and a lean, well-knit musculature. Yes, she could understand Othir's wistful interest, which Esmilinde clearly shared, as did Pavia and Rovina, who were eying him with longing from their posts by the two doors at the far end of the banquet hall. Observing his vaguely satirical smile, Sinta pondered whether this attractive young nobleman might be a murderer, or—more likely—an accomplice to murder.

Her reflections were interrupted by the last-minute arrival of Lord Anthilor and his wife Luria, the latter scolding like a fishwife.

"Damn it, woman, hold your tongue," he pleaded, as they entered the banquet hall. "We're here now, and we aren't late."

Sinta saw Luria catch herself up short, at the realization that she and her husband now had a sizeable audience. Lacking Othir's courtly training, Sinta may have failed to perceive the subtle lapses in taste marring the efforts of this rich merchant's daughter to dress like a fine lady, but there was no mistaking the inelegance of her carriage and deportment. As an apothecary's daughter herself, Sinta felt a pang of sympathy—though only a pang, for Luria made an unpleasant impression. Indeed, even from a distance, there was a hardness about the woman's expression that Sinta found worrying.

Anthilor and Luria had barely taken their seats when the prince and the princess-consort entered by their private door at the far left, along with the prince's bodyguard, Sir Thanifor, and the princess's confidante, Lady Mara. Conversation dutifully ceased, as everyone rose and bowed their heads.

Prince Folgar, Sinta reflected, was a man of remarkably unexceptional appearance: neither handsome nor ugly, tall nor short, fat nor thin. His intellect was similarly undistinguished, though she had to grant that he possessed the rare humility to recognize his own limitations—hence his reliance on Chancellor Thennis, which left him free to devote his time to riding, hunting, and losing modest sums at cards.

Princess Mirelde, the daughter of the Duke of Mar-Foreltir, was a good match for her husband in both intellect and temperament, and—so far as Sinta had heard—their marriage was a successful one. Although the princess-consort had by now lost such fragile prettiness as she once possessed, she had succeeded in her primary duty of producing an heir to the throne, leaving her free to devote her time to needlework, gossip, and the latest fashion in lapdogs.

The princely couple took their seats at the head of the table, and a careless gesture from Folgar gave the guests permission to resume their own. Pavia and Rovina broke the seals on several waiting bottles of a dry Hrissic white wine, extracted the corks, and worked their way down the table, serving each diner with an aperitif.

The conversation quickly turned to plans for an upcoming chase, with Folgar questioning his Master of the Hunt, a healthy specimen of middle years whose name Sinta could not recall, though she knew him by sight. Sir Thigtonil, whose successor as Master of the Horse had not yet been selected, weighed in as well, causing Sinta to sit up and take notice. Othir had been right, she decided, in describing him as good-looking, though she found his manner unattractive. He was simultaneously obsequious toward the prince and slightly disdainful toward the Master of the Hunt. When Lord Anthilor, as Master of the Hounds, ventured a vacuous remark of his own, Thigtonil was downright scornful. Sinta watched a deep flush sweep over the young lord's face as the new Gentleman of the Chamber mocked His Serene Highness's "esteemed kennel-keeper." Thigtonil, she decided, was a bully, and the prince's bodyguard had been right about Anthilor: he might be a fool, but he had feelings like anyone else.

The door at the far right end of the hall opened to admit the server Tarilor with the prince's soup course, which he handed off gracefully to Sir Thigtonil, whose day it was to act as taster. Coming face-to-face with Rovina on his way back out, the boy blushed and the girl giggled.

Deferentially approaching the prince, Ghelnor whispered something in his ear and motioned to Sinta, who realized she would have to play out the cover story he had improvised for her a few minutes earlier. She got up and walked the length of the table to where Sir Thigtonil held Tarilor's silver tray, which bore a steaming bowl of onion soup topped with melted cheese, together with several thick slices of crusty white bread still warm from the oven. She uttered a brief incantation in the mystical language of wizardry, which was full of guttural consonants and glottal stops that gave it a particularly exotic sound. She then moved seamlessly into a gratuitous bit of sorcery that made the food glow softly for a moment, so as to make it more apparent that she had actually done something.

"This fare is now safe," she declared, before adding, with a hint of derision, "but by all means taste it, Sir Thigtonil. I have no wish to usurp your essential function."

Sensing more from the sorceress's tone than from her actual words that he had been insulted, Thigtonil found it was his turn to flush. Setting down the tray, he took a spoonful of soup and tore off a piece of bread. "Mmm," he enthused. "Your Serene Highness indeed chose his cook wisely!" He sat down and glared at Sinta, as she returned to her place at the other end of the table.

Servers entered bearing soup and bread for the rest of the room. After discreetly casting her wizarding spell to neutralize any poison in her own portion (Othir would have to take his chances with his), Sinta lost herself in the savor of the onion soup and fresh bread. Nor was she alone in being distracted. Conversation petered out across the table, as the diners devoted themselves to the simple pleasure of eating.

As the food disappeared, conversation gradually resumed, but in a fragmented fashion. Sinta had the misfortune to be seated next to the wife of a minor court functionary who seemed to think that the world at large must be eager to hear about her two small children, aged three and five. "Clever as monkeys, they are—at least, I've heard that monkeys are clever. I've never actually seen one. But perhaps you have some familiarity with monkeys, Mistress Sinta. I feel certain that as a sorceress you must know something about monkeys. Such exotic creatures!"

Sinta firmly disclaimed any experience with monkeys, adding—in the vain hope of shutting the woman up—that she preferred lizards.

"Lizards? Oh, my! But those are reptiles, aren't they? I don't think I would like to own a lizard."

"They are not for everyone," Sinta conceded, frowning. "Much like small children!"

Further up the table, the unfaithful Esmilinde was batting her pretty eyelashes at Sinta's supremely uninterested man-at-arms. "So, who do *you* think committed the murders, Sir Othir?" Evidently she had gotten over the loss of Lord Alfron and felt ready to look for a replacement.

Othir opted to play dumb. "I have no idea, madam," he replied. "Mistress Sinta and I were in Tserenets when his lordship was poisoned and still on our way home when the court sorcerer was slain. I'm afraid we know little of the particulars."

"A woman will have been behind it, mark my words!" asserted Sir Topassin, with a disapproving glance at his wife. "Poison's a woman's weapon, after all."

"Perhaps," said Othir, "but wasn't the sorcerer stabbed to death?"

"In his bed—all the more reason to think the killer was a woman. A crime of passion, without doubt! Some hot-blooded southerner, I wouldn't be surprised."

"Poisoning doesn't seem very hot-blooded to me," objected a gangly young man, whom Othir recognized as the son of the prince's chamberlain. "Are we even sure the same person committed both crimes?"

"Let's not talk about such gruesome things," pleaded a dark-haired woman further up the table. "I'm sure I won't sleep a wink tonight, thinking about poisonings and stabbings and vicious murderers lurking undetected in our very midst!"

The diners in Othir's vicinity obligingly turned the conversation to the presumably less distressing topic of bear-baiting.

The servers soon returned to remove the empty soup bowls, after which Pavia and Rovina served an excellent Inirochian red wine to tide the company over until the main course. Sinta's neighbor was unaccountably reminded of something darling her little Thigvia had said that morning, leading her by some further impenetrable association of ideas to relate how talented little Thagvar was at singing Asardian hymns. "They really are both the sweetest little angels!" she exclaimed.

Sinta felt tempted to introduce the topic of prophetic dreams, so that she could claim to have had one in which the populace went mad and drowned their small children like kittens, but her good nature got the better of her, encouraged by her recollection that the royal couple's youngest daughter was only six. Instead, she sought to redirect the conversation at her end of the table by seeking enlightenment from Sir Rodor on certain points of falconry.

Tarilor now returned with the prince's main course—an enormous slab of venison, garnished with fresh rosemary and thyme, served with bread dumplings and roast mushrooms. Sinta again neutralized any poison that might have been present. The other servers brought venison for the rest of the company, and Sinta again took her own precautions. She did not often have the opportunity to eat venison, let alone venison prepared by a master such as Shingach. Conversation lagged for a good while, until most of the food was gone, at which point the prince asked his captain of the guard a question about the training of some newly recruited guardsmen, and Lord Caador was pulled briefly into the discussion. Lady Hrinde then began a conversation about the gross inadequacy of the servant class, a subject on which there seemed to be widespread agreement. Sinta considered this topic unnecessarily tactless, given the presence of Pavia and Rovina, but she thought it wiser to say nothing, rather than call further attention to herself by registering dissent.

After the servers removed the dirty dishes, conversation in the hall again fragmented. Sinta consented to answer questions about lizards from a young man several seats away, who expressed an interest in them, while Othir chatted hopefully with a nice-looking knight, who proved, however, to be disappointingly stupid. Dessert was then served, in the form of custard tarts of exceptional artistry, and the meal concluded with a blackberry liqueur, served as a digestif, after which the princely couple bade everyone a good evening and departed, followed in short order by their now sated guests.

❦

"I hope it wasn't a mistake to attend," Sinta remarked, as she and Othir made their way across the long bridge connecting castle and town. "Lord Caador wasn't fooled as to our purpose, and I doubt he was the only one."

"Perhaps," conceded Othir, "but you have to wonder if that meal wasn't worth it!"

12

An Ondiric nobleman's wife and children bear the courtesy titles of Lord or Lady, but only his eldest son inherits the nobleman's substantive title (baron, count, etc.) and with it the right to extend courtesy titles to his own wife and children.

—*A Guide to the Uses and Practices of the Ondiric Nobility*

Upon returning to the apothecary's shop, Sinta cast several additional wards on the already well-protected building to inconvenience any would-be murderous intruders, however they might attempt to gain access. She and Othir then retired to her study to review their investigation.

Sinta fed her pet lizard, Angvar, a grub and stroked his smooth, cool scales. "We have provisionally excluded a few people from suspicion," she noted (having no notion of the importance the least-likely suspect would assume in later Ondiric detective fiction), "and we have established strong motives for several others, but let us stipulate that we have failed, so far, to find anything suggesting that any of these people were capable of carrying out a magical poisoning, or knew anyone—excepting Halifor himself—who could have carried one out for them." She paused. "We still need to speak with this—" (she consulted her notes) "—Ghiron about potentially suspicious patterns of fruit consumption among the courtiers, but I have my doubts that we will find any."

Othir made an indistinct throaty noise that Sinta interpreted as expressing a shared skepticism on this score.

"The widow, Lady Hrinde, had a compelling motive to poison the cheating swine," Sinta continued, her distaste for the victim clouding her objectivity for a moment, "and she seems no less likely than anyone else to have found someone to brew a magical poison for her. Her whereabouts at the critical moment are unknown. Plus, she seems like a horrible person. Am I forgetting anything?"

"Only the question of why she would have waited this long to rid herself of him," Othir pointed out. "He'd been cheating on her for years, probably for the entirety of their marriage. Was there some precipitating event that would explain why now?"

Sinta made a note. "Yes, we should look into that." She pursed her lips. "Are we agreed that Alfron's son, Frildar, appears to have had no motive to kill his father, as well as no real capacity to carry out the poisoning?"

Othir nodded. "While I could imagine someone entangling him in a plot to kill Alfron, Frildar has neither the brains nor the initiative to be the moving force behind it, and since he was present in the banquet hall that day, we know he didn't deliver the poison himself."

Sinta consulted her notes again. "Sir Topassin certainly had a motive, and he threatened to gut Alfron like a fish!"

Othir conceded this. "Still, I think the servants were right that he would have done just that, gutted him, rather than use poison."

"Agreed. At the same time, he seemed eager tonight to direct suspicion elsewhere, and we don't know where he was when the poisoning occurred. So, he remains under suspicion." Sinta sighed. "That brings us to Sir Rodor, the prince's falconer, whom I rather like, so I don't want him to be guilty, but he did have a motive, and he knows something about natural poisons, so if we find out that he'd been stockpiling apricots or the like, things will look bad for him."

"He was in the banquet hall, though," Othir pointed out, "so he would have needed a confederate to deliver the poison. We know it wasn't his assistant, so who would it have been?"

"That is a problem," acknowledged Sinta. "He's a widower, so there's no wife to consider. Besides, isn't he the sort who would want to do the deed himself? That also argues against his hiring an assassin to kill Halifor. Furthermore, I'm not sure he would have had Halifor killed just for snooping around. Somehow I don't think someone who works with raptors for a living would lose his nerve like that."

"Who's next?" asked Othir.

"Anthilor, since he was the man who seemed most likely to get Alfron's job. Surely we're in agreement that he's too stupid to fall under serious suspicion of being the mastermind behind a poisoning plot. Additionally, he was in the banquet hall, so he would have needed to arrange for someone else to administer the poison for him."

Othir nodded. "Anthilor is mentally negligible. I refuse to consider him a likely suspect."

"What about his wife, Luria? She seems like a hard case, and once Alfron was dead, she campaigned for her husband's appointment in his place."

"She could have done it. Or she and Anthilor could have done it together. But she was in the banquet hall, too, so they still would have needed a confederate."

Sinta frowned. "Then there are Anthilor's parents, the Baron and Baroness of Toth. They sound pretty cold-blooded" (she stroked Angvar apologetically), "but would they really have been so set on creating a potential vacancy for him that they killed a man with whom they had no other quarrel?"

"People have killed for less," Othir observed. "And the baroness did leave the hall in time to poison the pork tenderloin. Besides, we don't know anything about their relationship with Alfron. Maybe they hated him!"

"Hmm. We should definitely look into that possibility." Sinta made a note. "There's also their son, Lord Caador. He could have done it, either on his own, or at their behest. He's got the brains, and as a soldier he's presumably made his peace with the need to kill people from time to time."

Othir sighed, unable to disagree. "Still, the motive of helping his brother seems a bit thin to me. I don't have the impression they're close."

Sinta glanced over her remaining notes. "Fortunately, I think we can safely ignore the rest of the people we investigated today. Lady Tisvena seems to have been broken-hearted rather than enraged over being dumped, and she was crying in her room when the poisoning occurred.

We're told her family didn't care about her troubles. Sir Rildan and his wife had no motive. Lady Floria appears to be too much of a nitwit to commit the crime, and her family didn't even know about her affair with Alfron, so they wouldn't have wanted him dead."

"I believe that characterizing Floria as a 'nitwit' is giving her too much credit," submitted Othir, helping himself to a hazelnut from a dish Sinta kept on her desk.

The sorceress tidied her notes, which now covered several sheets of parchment in her careful, minute handwriting. "Tomorrow we'll talk to Sir Thigtonil's man. Maybe he will know something useful."

Sinta had no way of knowing it, but that interview would lead the investigation in a disturbing new direction.

13

Plots and conspiracies were a recurring feature of court life in medieval Ondiran, particularly in the smaller sovereignties, where there was the least at stake.

> —*Form and Function: An Administrative History of the Predecessor States of the Province of Sindegorn*

The next day dawned rainy, making for an unpleasant walk to the castle. Sinta decided to begin the morning by visiting Ghiron, the court's balding, middle-aged produce czar, but his information, as expected, was unhelpful. He knew nothing about the poisoning of Lord Alfron beyond the fact that it had occurred. No one had requested any undue quantities of stone fruit from him. No one had stolen any discernible quantity of stone fruit. No one had behaved in a suspicious manner with regard to stone fruit. Sinta gave up and let him return to his duties procuring, inventorying, and dispensing stone fruit, along with other produce.

Sir Thigtonil's valet, Ksotir, would have been a fairly good-looking young man, but for a distinctly self-satisfied expression and a pair of shifty eyes. He also had the misfortune to suffer from a marked limp, owing to a badly set broken leg in childhood. All the body servants Sinta and Othir had interviewed were well dressed, but Ksotir stood out for his relative sartorial splendor, which even ran to a crushed velvet collar.

Something about him prompted Sinta to put a little extra power into her charm spell—just to be on the safe side.

Although Ksotir did not know who poisoned Lord Alfron, or where his master was at the time, he could attest that Thigtonil was delighted about the sudden vacancy at court and that his political faction sprang immediately into action to secure his appointment as Gentleman of the Chamber. "It was all very hush-hush," Ksotir recalled, "with lots of whispered conversations and secret meetings." The self-satisfied look on his face intensified. "The master trusted me to carry all kinds of secret messages to his supporters."

"Which you read, of course," Othir interjected.

"Well, sure, I tried to, but I couldn't break the wax seals without getting caught."

Despite a pair of sharp ears and an inclination to listen at doors, Ksotir remained largely ignorant of the wider goals of Thigtonil's faction, though he knew its members disapproved of Thennis's leadership as chancellor. Asked point blank if he suspected them of having murdered Lord Alfron, he replied, "I can't say, but it sure seems likely, don't it?"

Sinta pressed him for names.

"The master's friends Lord Donaril and Sir Hrogan, of course—they're thick as thieves, they are—and Lord Torvil, the Eighth Baron of Ferigan—he's the real bigwig, the big shot, the big cheese—and Sir Hrogan's wife, Fildenea—she's got a man's brains, that one—I wouldn't be surprised if she knew a thing or two about poisons." He paused. "And there's Sir Fainor, first assistant to the treasurer—he's on their side, too."

Ksotir didn't think anyone in Thigtonil's faction could do magic—Sir Thigtonil certainly couldn't—but who could say what connections some of them might have in the wider world? Lord Torvil, for example, was a baron, after all.

After sending Ksotir away, Sinta turned to Othir for possible guidance regarding this largely new cast of characters. "I didn't like the sound of that," she added. "Quite apart from whether this faction is connected to the murders, Thennis is a good chancellor, and he doesn't need his political enemies embedding themselves in the prince's inner circle." She began to wonder if his uncharacteristic disquiet the day he came to the apothecary's shop had been due to the killings alone.

Othir took out the assassin's magic dagger and thrust it at an imaginary target, hoping to persuade it to accept him as its new owner. "You will remember that Lord Torvil, the Baron of Ferigan—Ksotir's 'big cheese'—is Lady Tisvena's father. As I told you yesterday, he and his wife are immoderately wealthy, due in large part to her landholdings in Menfir and his mining interests in Fendoran. Thennis was worried about possible foreign involvement. Perhaps he was right to be."

Sinta frowned. "What about this Lord Donaril person?"

Othir shook his head. "One of the younger sons of the Baron of Hront. He's been hanging around the court lately, hoping to secure an appointment, but I gather he made a poor impression on the prince, so he hasn't gotten one. I'm not surprised to learn that he's attached himself to a group that's dissatisfied with the current arrangements."

Sinta consulted her notes. "He wasn't at the banquet hall on the day Alfron was poisoned. What about Sir Hrogan and his wife?"

"He has some minor appointment—inspecting the castle's privies, or something equally demeaning. I'm sure he's hoping Sir Thigtonil can persuade the prince to give him something better. I don't know much about his wife, except that between the two of them, she seems to have the brains."

"Let's see—neither one was at the banquet hall. And Sir Fainor? He *was* there, along with his wife."

Othir nodded. "He's rather like Sir Thigtonil—energetic, ambitious, and impatient—a climber. He trained as a lawyer, I believe, and works for the court treasurer. If you ask me, Fainor's a lean and hungry fellow who has the potential to be dangerous."

Sinta jotted down some additional notes. "And Fainor's wife? What do you know about her?"

Othir shrugged. “Lady Tersa? She’s daughter to the Baron of Hront, which makes her Lord Donaril’s sister. No doubt that’s how Fainor first found his way into Thigtonil’s circle of friends. Tersa’s very quiet and opts to stay in the background, but I happened to chat with her once. She’s not stupid.”

Sinta sighed. More suspects but no hard evidence!

Having ascertained from Ghelnor that the Baron and Baroness of Ferigan did not happen to be visiting Talindor at the moment with their servants, Sinta opted to summon Sir Fainor’s valet and Lady Tersa’s maid. They were a study in contrast. Fin, the valet, with his slicked-down hair and wispy moustache, had the cocky air of a young man on the make, while Agara, the maid, exuded respectability, having served her mistress’s baronial family since before her ladyship was born. Once charmed, he had a good deal to say, while she radiated disapproval of her louche companion and said little.

Both servants denied knowledge of the poisoning, though Fin suspected the Baron of Toth and his wife. “They wanted Lord Alfron’s position for that numbskull son of theirs, but Sir Thigtonil gave ’em a surprise, didn’t he? He had Lord Torvil on his side! The prince’s a big believer in old noble families, you know, so he’s gonna trust an eighth baron over a second baron any day of the week—especially if the guy’s rich as sin! At least, that’s what the master says, and he’s a clever man, he is. I mean, not only does he do all right out of that treasury job of his, he's way too smart for them to catch him with his hand in the till."

Agara sniffed indignantly but said nothing.

Sinta made a note to mention Fainor's alleged peculation to Thennis and then asked for more details about the efforts to promote Thigtonil's candidacy.

Fin's account corresponded roughly to Ksotir's: Lord Alfron's death occasioned great excitement among Sir Thigtonil's friends; there were secret messages and hushed conversations; from what Fin could gather, the plotters were working to gain influence over the prince and undermine Thennis.

Agara averred that the master should be ashamed of himself for taking part in such a disgraceful intrigue, prompting Fin to laugh and say that women did not understand politics.

Suppressing an eye roll, Sinta asked whether Sir Fainor or anyone connected to him or his friends knew anything about poisons.

Agara said that she had overheard Sir Hrogan's wife, Fildenea, explaining to the mistress that arsenic was the best way to destroy rats and mice.

Fin submitted that Fildenea was the sort of female who *would* know about things like that. Not a true gentlewoman, that one!

Sinta resisted the urge to throw a spell inducing Fin to wet himself. Instead, she continued with her line of questions. Did any of these people know how to do magic, or have connections to magicians?

Fin nodded vigorously. “The master’s got a cousin who’s a sorcerer. Flimflamtinor or Flinflantinator, some goofy name like that. The guy’s got a creepy pet lizard, of all things!”

Othir tried but failed to suppress a laugh.

Sinta shot him a look. “Has this cousin visited recently? Or has Sir Fainor visited him?”

Fin nodded again. “Yeah, the master and I went to see him in Brix about a month ago. The master wanted him to do some spell or other for him, I think. I don’t know what it was.”

The town of Brix in the Duchy of Mar-Beran was located some six leagues northwest of Fendor. Sinta was surprised that she had not heard of a sorcerer practicing there. Further questioning established, however, that this Flimflamtinor or Flinflantinator had only just moved to the town, after finishing his apprenticeship.

As Fin and Agara were leaving, Fin volunteered that during the visit to Brix the lizard had bitten him on the finger after he poked it.

“Lizards will do that,” Sinta advised sternly. “It’s better to leave them be.”

“I’m a little concerned that all the conspiring seems to have come *after* Alfron’s death,” Sinta remarked to Othir, as they waited for Ghelnor to bring their lunch up to the chancellory, “but I suppose the plan to poison him could have been more closely held.”

"I wouldn't trust any of those people with it," said Othir. "I would just make it happen and then rally my forces to take advantage."

"I'll keep that in mind, should the occasion arise," Sinta replied drily. She got up to stretch her legs. "I'll have to ask Valdira about this sorcerer in Brix. She may know whether he's the kind of person to hand out magical poisons to his relatives without a second thought."

❦

After lunch, they interviewed Sir Hrogan's man, Marto, and Fildenea's maid, Thilba. Marto was Tseren, but he spoke Ondiric with native fluency, while Thilba was a local girl. Both were in their early twenties and attractive in an understated way. Sinta quickly sensed that they were engaged in a covert romance, but she saw no need to embarrass them by asking any questions that would bring their relationship out into the open.

Sir Hrogan's appointment proved to be as Keeper of the Princely Library, a position Sinta refused to consider demeaning at all, let alone comparable to inspecting the castle's privies, but both servants insisted that Sir Hrogan felt it to be a humiliation. The prince's collection contained few volumes, all accessioned prior to the current reign, and His Serene Highness had not yet seen fit to consult any of them during Sir Hrogan's tenure, which had now stretched to two years. Nor had Sir Hrogan himself, for that matter.

His wife, Fildenea, the daughter of a mid-level municipal official, was impatient for her husband to advance.

Thilba was not sure she knew about poisons, but they seemed like the kind of thing the mistress, who was practical and clever, would know about. After all, *she* spent time reading in the prince's library. Neither servant, however, had any reason to think either the master or the mistress knew anyone who could do magic.

They were not certain where Sir Hrogan and his wife were at the relevant time, though Marto believed they had probably been out riding. He had a clear memory, however, of the master hearing the news of Lord Alfron's death from Sir Thigtonil. "He certainly seemed surprised, miss, and Sir Thigtonil was excited. I didn't have the impression that either of them had a hand in it, but Sir Thigtonil had definite hopes that his lordship, the Baron of Ferigan, would persuade His Serene Highness to appoint him in Lord Alfron's place, as of course happened."

Sinta asked about their attitude toward Chancellor Thennis.

"Oh, they don't like him, miss, but the main thing is that they expect their fortunes to rise, if his lordship succeeds in ousting him and becoming chancellor himself."

Apprised of these developments, Thennis sighed and put down his quill. "Torvil and I have clashed on policy and personnel ever since he inherited the barony upon his father's death. That must be sixteen years ago now. Well, he and his friends have every right to oust me if they can, so long as they don't murder anyone along the way. Or collude treasonously with a rival power." He fixed Sinta with a skeptical eye. "I take it that you have yet to uncover any proof of either potentiality?"

Sinta admitted that she had not. "But we haven't been able to interview the baron's servants yet, since they're attending him on his estate in Ferigan."

Thennis granted that this was a fair point. "I'll arrange a pretext for him to attend some court function here in Talindor. That will bring the servants to you."

Having no court appointment, Sir Thigtonil's friend Lord Donaril did not live at the castle, but the efficient Ghelnor was able to establish where he was lodging. In the process, he happened to spot the man himself skulking in one of the castle courtyards, complaining to another disappointed office-seeker about the endemic corruption that kept worthy fellows like themselves from obtaining lucrative posts. The coast was therefore clear for Sinta and Othir to go interview his valet, along with—as it turned out—his landlord and a downtrodden housemaid.

The standard of accommodation suggested that Lord Donaril received an ample allowance from his father, the Baron of Hront. The valet, a plump little man named Mur, confirmed that his lordship had money to spare (not, the maid interjected bitterly, that the rich weasel ever chose to spare any).

Sinta asked about Lord Alfron's death and the excitement it seemed to have generated in Lord Donaril's circle. Mur recalled that Sir Thigtonil's man, Ksotir (at whose name the maid snorted with disgust), had come to the house that day to fetch his lordship urgently to the castle. Whatever the nature of this summons, his lordship did not return until late in the night. The landlord confirmed Mur's account, but none of the three could recall any suspicious circumstances prior to Lord Alfron's death. Mur denied that Lord Donaril would know anything about poisons or magic, though his lordship's father, the Baron of Hront, was friendly with a sorcerer in the Free City of Nimdir.

Finally, Sinta asked about any contact Lord Donaril might have had with possible foreign agents, such as the five envoys resident in Talindor. Neither servant knew of any, but Mur pointed out that he had very little insight into what his lordship did when he went up to the castle, and the maid aired her view that his lordship was just the sort of crooked character who would take foreign money, if it were on offer.

"I'm not sure we're getting any closer to finding the poisoner," Sinta admitted, as she and Othir trudged back to the apothecary's shop through a thin drizzle, "but we still have leads to follow—and if nothing else, I'd like to think we'll manage to break up this little conspiracy to get rid of Chancellor Thennis."

14

Avoid introducing *too* many red herrings, lest you reduce your readers—or worse yet, yourself—to a state of abject confusion.

—*The Art of Mystery Writing*
(Ondiric Authors' Guild How-to Series, vol. 6)

That evening, Sinta wrote a letter to Valdira, asking for information about a journeyman sorcerer in Brix, improbably named Flimflamtinor or Flinflantinator, and an unnamed sorcerer in Nimdir, who was reportedly friends with the Baron of Hront. Once the missive was drafted, she used the teleportation spell in *Djanko's Grimoire* to drop it on the desk in her mentor's study. Teleporting things—not to speak of people—to places one could not see was risky, but Sinta reckoned that the only danger here was that the clutter on Valdira's desk might prevent one extra sheet of parchment from coming to her immediate notice. To reduce the chances of such a mishap, she first rolled the letter up and then tied it with a bright red ribbon that she enchanted to emit a throbbing glow.

Although Sinta then retired to bed, she had difficulty falling asleep, as her thoughts turned back to Halifor. The demands of the investigation had allowed her to distract herself, to some extent, from the pain of losing him, and the funeral had provided some catharsis, but the grief was still there, a dark cloud that now enveloped her thoughts, as she tossed and turned, recalling with sad affection both his merits and his flaws. Sinta did not have an excessive number of friends, and she bitterly resented any reduction in their ranks. Also contributing to her sleeplessness was a heightened concern for her own safety, following dinner the night before. Whoever had thought it necessary to have Halifor murdered might now be plotting the same fate for her, as well, just to be on the safe side. Selfish though it might seem, Sinta had no wish to be killed.

The next morning she was somewhat cheered to find a reply from Valdira, tied with a yellow ribbon that was twittering and trilling like an impassioned goldfinch:

My dear Sinta [the missive began],

I have not yet made the acquaintance of the new sorcerer in Brix (who I believe is correctly called Flantinor), but he trained under my friend Nerithin, whom I consider unlikely to have featured magical poisons any more prominently in his curriculum than I did in yours.

I believe the sorcerer in Nimdir to whom you refer must be Voldar. I do not know him personally, but judging from his reputation I would say his skill exceeds his scruples. I therefore counsel you to be wary of him.

Good luck with your investigation. Please convey my regards to the dashing Sir Othir.

Yours affectionately,

V.

P.S. Little Haldor is beginning to pick up his first words in Tseren!

Sinta shared the letter with Othir over breakfast. "We'll have to keep this fellow Voldar in mind," she told him, "but I don't think the anti-Thennis faction would have procured the poison from a friend of the father of one of its least impressive conspirators. It's too roundabout. I'd wager instead that Lord Torvil had his own means of acquiring a magical poison. As that smug little sneak Ksotir put it, he is a baron, after all."

The previous day's rain continued, now with occasional flashes of lightning and rumbles of thunder. Unable, as yet, to question Lord Torvil's retainers, Sinta and Othir spent their time interviewing a multitude of footmen, housemaids, hallboys, and sundry other servants who worked in and around the castle. Fishing for clues in a vast sea of idle speculation, random facts, and uninformed commentary, they had a frustrating time. Several servants expounded wild theories, blaming the prince, or the princess-consort, or Thennis for the murders, while others were convinced a dark religious conspiracy was at play, centering upon the Hrintic exarch in Mindor. "He has his agents everywhere!" one of the laundresses warned, apparently referring to the many Hrintic priests and lay preachers who were active throughout eastern Ondiran.

A few of the servants, however, had seen or heard something relevant, though their information did not always lead anywhere in particular. One of the chamber-maids, for example, was able to identify another of Alfron's former paramours for them—a lady-in-waiting who had a brief fling with him three years earlier—but the woman had subsequently made a highly advantageous marriage and moved away to the Principality of Ool, so there seemed little reason to suspect her.

More helpful were the interviews that established people's whereabouts at the time of the poisoning. One of the grooms was thus able to confirm that Sir Hrogan and his wife, Fildenea, had in fact gone out riding well before the hullabaloo over Lord Alfron started and returned well after it. He had saddled their horses for them and saw them depart and return. They went out riding most days at about that time, if the weather was fair, so there was nothing unusual about their doing so on this occasion. They always took a basket along that he assumed to be a picnic meal.

One of the housemaids, similarly, was able to attest that Lord Alfron's widow, Lady Hrinde, could not have administered the poison, because she was otherwise occupied at the time, "screaming blue murder at me for not cleaning the bedchamber to her ladyship's satisfaction." Evidently the opprobrium and abuse flowed freely for quite some time. Lady Hrinde had just seized the girl's broom and struck her with it, when a pageboy arrived, breathless, with the news of Lord Alfron's death. "Her ladyship was thunderstruck—she really was," the maid recalled. "She dropped my broom and stared at the boy like he was crazy. 'I hope he suffered,' she said, finally. 'That bastard didn't deserve to die quick.'"

Several servants admitted to being glad that visits to the castle by Lord Torvil and his wife were infrequent, as the two were haughty, impatient, and unforgiving. While his lordship was said to be a clever man, he had the temper of a demon. And while her ladyship might be distant kin to the Count of Menfir, the fat cow acted as though she were a countess herself.

Finally, a few people confessed to having a superstitious fear of the Baroness of Toth. "Things happen to folk who get on her bad side," explained one of the hallboys, a lad of thirteen with a bad case of acne. "She didn't like the way I cleaned her shoes, and my face broke out the next day. Rem the farrier talked back to her once and then got kicked by a mule."

Othir was unimpressed by such trivial coincidences, but Sinta made a note of them all the same.

❖

"Lord Torvil and his wife will be here tomorrow," Thennis announced, as his two sleuths prepared to leave for the day. "Ghelnor will see to it that their servants are quietly delivered unto you."

Sinta nodded absently, her mind still working through the day's rich haul of largely irrelevant rubbish. "Oh, yes, thank you, Your Excellency," she said, suddenly realizing that he had spoken. "I'm sure that will be very helpful."

Othir grinned. "And even if it isn't, I suspect we'll hear some interesting gossip!"

15

Medieval city life was full of dangers, not least those posed by criminal gangs specializing in robbery, mayhem, and murder for hire.

Crime and Punishment in Medieval Ondiran

Pelted with rain from angry clouds, Sinta and Othir descended the castle hill and crossed the bridge into the city. They had scarcely entered the latter's narrow streets on their way home to the apothecary's shop, when they passed a shabbily dressed but brawny man sheltering from the downpour in a shallow doorway. Sinta did not like the look of him but reassured herself that he seemed focused more on staying dry than on molesting passing pedestrians. Othir, she noticed, cautiously shifted his hand to the hilt of his sword all the same.

The sorceress and her man-at-arms were just reaching the next corner, when a sharp whistle sounded behind them. Twisting around, Sinta saw that the brawny man was now advancing toward them with a heavy hammer in his hand. At the same time, four confederates answered his signal by stepping abruptly out from the intersecting street, two from either side. Three of these men had weapons out —a dagger, a hatchet, and a bludgeon—while the fourth carried a nozzled cow's bladder and wore a knife at his belt. Sinta and Othir had walked into an ambush.

A flash of lightning briefly illuminated the attackers' thuggish faces, followed almost immediately by a deafening thunderclap. Othir had already drawn his sword and was reaching for his dagger, too, when the man with the bladder pointed the nozzle at him and squeezed a vile stream of mud and ordure into his face. With a sputtering oath, Othir swung blindly in his assailant's general direction, missing wide, after which the man with the bludgeon darted in to hit the befouled knight in the chest, as he attempted to wipe the filth from his eyes. Fortunately, it was only a glancing blow, and the padding under Othir's enchanted hauberk cushioned the impact somewhat.

Sinta, caught by surprise, was forced into close combat before she could cast any spells. By lucky chance, the act of turning to look behind her had saved her from a dagger thrust that missed only because the sorceress's slender waist presented an even narrower target in profile than it did from the front. She struck back as best she could, though the awkward angle against a close opponent deprived her of both momentum and leverage. She managed nonetheless to bring the quarterstaff down on his head—not nearly as hard as she would have liked, but hard enough to stagger him, after which he obligingly slipped on the wet cobblestones and fell, flailing, to the ground. Sinta would have liked to follow up with a more decisive attack, but she was too busy dodging a blow from the thug with the hatchet, while also planting one iron-shod end of her quarterstaff firmly in the midsection of the man with the hammer, knocking the wind out of him as he ran up behind them.

Othir had both weapons drawn now. Neither magic blade was making it easy for him, but his unarmored opponents were wise to be wary of them even so. His long dagger grudgingly consented to deflect a second blow from the thug with the bludgeon, even as his uncooperative sword thrust harmlessly past the other man, who had dropped the bladder and was pulling out his knife. Frustrated, Othir used his mail-clad elbow instead to bloody the nose of the latter individual, who fumbled and dropped the knife. Using both sword and dagger to keep the man with the bludgeon at bay, Othir kicked the fallen knife well behind himself and out of its owner's reach.

Sinta thrust her quarterstaff hard into the groin of the man with the hatchet, for Colmar had impressed upon her the utmost importance, when fighting for one's life, of doing whatever was necessary to win. The unfortunate thug doubled over with an agonized gasp, enabling Sinta to hit him again, this time in the knee. There was a nasty cracking sound, as his patella fractured, and down he went. Seeing that the man with the dagger was about to regain his feet, Sinta swung the other end of her staff around, bringing it down onto his head, this time with full momentum, concussing him. That left the brawny man with the hammer, who had evidently recovered from her previous blow to his solar plexus. As the wind threw rain in the man's face, Sinta feinted to his left, then struck a stinging blow to his right wrist that made him drop the hammer.

"Arrgh!" he roared, grabbing hold of her quarterstaff with his left hand. "I've had enough of this shit from you, little girl." Seemingly oblivious to any lingering pain in his wrist, he clamped his right hand onto the staff as well. With nearly twice Sinta's weight and considerably more upper-body strength, he was able to wrench the weapon out of her hands, yanking her violently toward him—and nearly off her feet—in the process. Throwing the staff to the ground, he grabbed the unhappy sorceress by the throat and began to throttle her.

Othir was busy facing off against the thug with the bludgeon, while his other opponent scrambled to pick up the dagger and the hatchet that Sinta's attackers had dropped. Once again Othir used his own dagger to fend off the bludgeon, while also slashing with his petulant sword. The latter, which should have buried itself deep in the flank of Othir's foe, merely grazed him instead, drawing blood but not incapacitating the man.

"Damn it!" Othir shouted. "Obey me or I'll have you melted down!" Swinging hard at the wounded thug, he struck him brutally on the thigh—despite the sword's continuing reluctance—cleaving muscle and sinew all the way to the bone. The man with the bludgeon screamed, staggered, and fell, clutching his leg. The other man threw the hatchet at Othir, but when it missed, he turned and ran, rather than attack a knight in chainmail while armed with nothing more than a dagger.

Terrified and unable to breathe, Sinta struggled desperately, as the burly man hoisted her into the air. She managed to unsheathe the magic knife at her belt, but using it was not so easy, partly because her opponent had a longer reach than she did, but chiefly because he was choking the life out of her. Finally, she succeeded in driving the blade upward into his left bicep, breaking his grip. He dropped her rather heavily to the ground, where she lay, gasping for breath, while he swore and retrieved his fallen hammer. With the last of her strength, Sinta summoned up a simple spell. Out of the corner of her eye, she saw Othir coming to her aid, but before he could reach her, and just as the burly man was raising the hammer above his head, she gestured wordlessly, and her assailant collapsed onto the cobblestones, sound asleep.

Sinta looked up at Othir, who was still plastered with muck, the pouring rain notwithstanding. She gave a feeble giggle that ended in a cough. "Poor Othir," she whispered hoarsely. "And you thought getting a face full of pepper was bad!"

Chancellor Thennis expressed dismay at the battered condition of his two investigators. "And you're certain this was a deliberate murderous attack, not an attempted robbery gone wrong?"

"Yes, Your Excellency," replied Othir. "It was an ambush, and their clear intent was to kill us."

"My fault," Sinta croaked, her voice raw from her recent brush with strangulation. "We shouldn't have dined in the banquet hall. Gave the game away."

Thennis summoned the court healer—a talented person who often visited the apothecary's shop—to tend to their injuries; Othir was allowed—indeed, encouraged—to bathe, and some clean clothes were found for him to borrow; Sinta tried but failed to find the strength to cast a spell to cleanse his armor; and Ghelnor was sent to fetch Master Siv, Talindor's public executioner, whose duties included interrogating criminal suspects.

The healer applied a salve to the ugly bruises encircling Sinta's neck, as well as the one blossoming on Othir's chest. She also ordered that a hot medicinal beverage, sweetened with honey, be brought to soothe Sinta's throat. Turning to the captured thugs, she applied the same salve to their bruises and sprinkled some wine into their wounds, which she then bound up with linen bandages. The broken knee was more of a problem. She gently prodded the swollen joint—shushing the patient's anguished cries—to determine the severity of the break and shook her head. "Although I can put this in a cast, it is too badly broken to heal well."

"Do what you can," said Thennis, "but I don't think these men need concern themselves excessively with the long-term future."

Master Siv was a large, muscular, intimidating man with a disfiguring scar running down the left side of his face. He disliked his disreputable job as public hangman and judicial torturer, which he had inherited from his father and his father's father, but he disliked alleged criminals even more and had no pangs of conscience regarding the distasteful things he was asked to do to them, even if—truth be told—he much preferred working in his garden.

"Let me explain the situation to you fine fellows," he told the captured ruffians, once Othir and Sinta were done giving their account of the ambush. An autodidact, he had an unexpectedly fussy way of speaking. "We are about to commence a 'preliminary investigative interview'" (he removed some distinctly evil-looking instruments from a blood-stained bag), "during which I am not yet authorized to use these little persuaders of mine to impress upon you the wisdom—indeed, the urgency—of telling me the truth. You should therefore consider it your one and only chance to tell me the truth *before* I receive such authorization, which I assure you, will happen without fail on the morrow, should the authorities not be satisfied with your answers tonight." He held up a cruelly serrated blade. "You've heard what the two victims had to say. In contrast to your sorry selves, they are both respectable, law-abiding subjects of His Serene Highness—indeed, one is a knight of the realm. I hope none of you intends to insult my intelligence by denying your participation in the disgraceful attack they described."

Three of the prisoners shook their heads as emphatically as they could, given their various injuries. They knew Master Siv and his methods. Only the brawny man who had attempted to strangle Sinta chose instead to bare his teeth and look defiant.

Siv clucked his tongue. "You disappoint me, Bogir. No matter. You will be more forthcoming in the course of our sessions tomorrow." He gestured dismissively. "So, tell me, the rest of you, how this attack came about. Who was behind it? Who hired you?" He pointed to the thug who had carried the hatchet. "Proth, you first."

Proth shook his close-cropped head. "Weren't nobody we knew, Master Siv, I swear it. Tall guy of middle years, dressed like a gentleman in a fine red velvet cloak. Brown hair, brown eyes, brown mustache."

The thug who had attacked Sinta with a dagger broke in indignantly. "You're such a liar, Proth! He were young and short, and merchant-class by his clothes—though, yeah, he did speak like gentry. But his eyes was blue, not brown, and he were clean-shaven. He didn't have no mustache!"

The thug who had carried the bludgeon scoffed. "You're both crazy! He weren't neither tall nor short, just fat as a pig! And he had straw-colored hair, too, with a straw-colored cloak to match."

For his part, Bogir just shook his head disgustedly and said nothing.

Siv lost his temper. "Don't give me this stinking sparrowshit!" he bellowed. "All four of you boys are in for a fine time tomorrow, I'm telling you."

Sinta coughed. "I think there may be spellcraft behind this, Master Siv, not deception. There are magicks that will change a person's appearance diversely to all who see them. Useful if you don't want to be identified." She downed the last of the healer's medicine, which had long since gone cold. "I'd like to hear some details about how they were hired. Where and when did it happen? How much were they paid?"

Siv turned back to the prisoners. "You heard her! Start talking."

Proth hastened to cooperate. "It was this afternoon at the Scalded Pig," he said. "This guy comes in, and he seems to know who we are. Asks if we're interested in a sweet little job—a double hit, he sez. Some girl and her fancy man. There's one princely crown in it for each of you, he sez, half in advance, half after. Seemed like a good price."

"Yeah, that's right," exclaimed the thug whom Sinta had hit twice on the head, "but he didn't say the girl carried a big ole stick with her. And knew how to use it!"

"Nor that the man would have chainmail and two whackin' big swords, neither!" added the one with the bandaged thigh.

Proth nodded in vigorous agreement with them both. "Nah, he just said to make sure we caught 'em by surprise, 'cause the girl knew magic, and we shouldn't give her a chance to throw any spells."

Chancellor Thennis looked amused. "Most unfortunate. No doubt you would have a colorable legal claim for deceptive practices against this person—if only you knew who he was." (Bogir rolled his eyes and growled.) Thennis turned to Sinta and Othir. "As for the two of you, it has grown late, and I think it would perhaps be best if you spent the night here in the castle."

16

Lord Sivtorin, Seventh Count of Menfir, came to power after the death of his brother, the Sixth Count, under suspicious circumstances. His foreign policy was aggressive and his domestic policy oppressive, but he is now chiefly remembered for his patronage of the great sculptor Volorit of Torul. Sivtorin was assassinated by a disgruntled member of the gentry in the ninth year of his reign.

—*Who Was Who in Medieval Ondiran*

Neither Sinta nor Othir felt more than slightly recovered the next morning. Sinta's throat remained sore and her voice husky, while the bruise on Othir's chest ached persistently. Nevertheless, the night's sleep had restored most of Sinta's spell power, and Ghelnor accompanied her to the castle's dungeon early to test her theory that magic had confounded the prisoners' impressions of who had hired them. Her charm spells did indeed confirm that they genuinely believed their divergent descriptions of that person. Bogir even thought it had been an attractive woman with an unusually deep voice.

After breakfast, Sinta and Othir resumed interviewing miscellaneous servants, while they waited for Lord Torvil and his wife to arrive with theirs. Although they did not learn anything new or useful, Sinta's castings assured that they continued to receive the unvarnished opinions of the servant class regarding their so-called betters. The prince, they were told, was a "dolt," the princess-consort a "dingbat," Lady Hrinde a "harpy," Lord Anthilor a "nincompoop," Sir Thigtonil a "bootlicker," Sir Fainor a "crook," and the Baron of Toth a "prize bastard." Few members of the court came in for praise, though Chancellor Thennis was generally well regarded, and Sir Rodor, the falconer, was acknowledged to be a good fellow, even if his refusal to employ a valet drew censure. Pavia turned out not to be the only servant in the castle—of either sex—with a yen for the suave envoy from Mar-Tigret, and there were also several who secretly admired Sir Topassin's beautiful but unfaithful wife, Esmilinde. Not a few also expressed an interest in Othir, who seemed flattered by the attention.

After lunch, Ghelnor was finally able to escort the baron's valet and the baroness's maid to the chancellory, where Sinta promptly charmed them. Nithor, the valet, was old and frail, having dutifully served Lord Torvil's father and grandfather before him, making the Eighth Baron of Ferigan his own personal third baron. He had the hangdog expression of a man who has been persuaded that the abuse he has been dealt over the years was his rightful due, while Viltsa, the lady's maid, though young and healthy, had the haggard, bewildered look of an animal that does not understand why it is beaten.

Sinta began by asking whether either Lord Torvil or Lady Irolte had come to Talindor the day before, in time to hire the gang of thugs at the Scalded Pig, but both servants insisted that the master and mistress had been home all day and had traveled to the capital only in response to Thennis's summons. Nor could they recall any suspicious travel that might have been conducted to arrange Halifor's murder. Unsurprisingly, they had no personal knowledge of who poisoned Lord Alfron, though when pressed, both had to admit that they considered their employers capable of this or indeed almost any other crime. Being compelled to state their true opinions, however, obviously terrified them, in case word of it got back to the baron and his wife.

Regarding magic and magicians, Nithor was able to say that Lord Torvil was good friends with a sorcerer in Mar-Firth, but he was quite certain they had not seen one another in over a year, so it seemed unlikely that this man could have provided his lordship with a magical poison. He also knew that her ladyship had had an affair many years ago with a sorcerer in Torul, but his lordship had avenged this dishonor by stabbing the man in the back with a sword, killing him, so no magical poison could possibly have been procured from that source.

The mention of the city of Torul brought Sinta conveniently to the question of the couple's foreign interests. Nithor confirmed that her ladyship's landholdings in the County of Menfir were richer than his lordship's baronial estate at Ferigan, though his lordship's stake in one of the Fendoric tin mines came close to redressing the balance. Her ladyship was, in fact, from Menfir originally—indeed, she was fourth cousin to the count himself. It was a source of intense pride to her, although, as Nithor understood it, being fourth cousins meant all they shared was a single pair of great-great-great-grandparents. Nithor's anxiety about speaking frankly seemed gradually to be lessening, whereas Viltsa clearly preferred to let him do all the talking.

Sinta asked about the envoys from Menfir and Fendoran. Did the baron and his wife ever associate with them? Both servants nodded. Not the Fendoric one, Nithor noted, but the Menfiric envoy was a frequent visitor to the baron's castle, as was the envoy's confidential secretary. "They always seem to have a lot to talk about behind closed doors," he observed. "They don't want the likes of us servants listening in."

When Sinta asked about the flurry of activity surrounding Alfron's death, Nithor frowned. "Word came from Talindor that poor Lord Alfron had been poisoned, and his lordship got very excited. 'We must take advantage of this!' he declared and rode off to the capital by himself that same evening, leaving me to follow him, along with her ladyship, and Viltsa here, and one of the grooms, the next morning with the usual luggage, which Viltsa and I had to spend much of the night packing."

Sinta and Othir exchanged looks. By this account, it did not sound as though the baron had known about the poisoning in advance. Sinta followed up, but Nithor could remember no conspiratorial activity in the days leading up to Lord Alfron's death, though there had been lots of it in the days following. "His lordship wants to be chancellor, and he saw getting his friend Sir Thigtonil close to the prince as a big step in that direction."

"Was the Menfiric envoy or his secretary involved in any of that?" Othir asked sharply.

"Not so far as I know, sir," Nithor replied. "But I cannot say who the master spoke with on the night of Lord Alfron's death, when he rushed to the prince's castle alone." He paused. "Still, I do have the impression, sir, that the envoy would like to see his lordship topple Chancellor Thennis. Of course, I don't really understand such affairs of state, but surely his lordship would pursue a friendlier policy toward Menfir than does Chancellor Thennis."

After the interview, Sinta and Othir went to see the chancellor. "I don't believe Lord Torvil and his friends were behind the poisoning," Sinta told him. "They were quick to exploit it, but Lord Alfron's death seems to have caught them by surprise, and we haven't been able to show that any of them obtained the poison, let alone administered it. Nor do they seem implicated in Halifor's murder or in the attack on us last night. On the other hand, Torvil and his wife are closer to the Menfiric envoy than loyal subjects of Sildoor perhaps should be, so I won't be surprised if they turn out to have plotted with him against you." She explained the details of what she and Othir had learned. "I think an interview with the envoy's confidential secretary would quickly get us to the truth of the matter."

Thennis placed the tips of his long, thin fingers pensively together and gazed upward, contemplating the intricate pattern of shadows on the ceiling. "It is customary not to maltreat foreign diplomats," he said after a moment, "lest one's own diplomats be maltreated in turn, but if this secretary implicates Lord Torvil, it is Lord Torvil who will be punished. The secretary and his master will merely be expelled from Sildoor. If our own envoy in Torul is expelled from Menfir in retaliation, I think that is a price worth paying for the exposure of Lord Torvil's treason—if such it be." He turned to his clerk. "Ghelnor, see to it that the secretary is summoned here."

Thogril, the confidential secretary, was a youngish man, well groomed and tailored, with an intense, alert expression, who clearly would have preferred flirting with Othir to answering dangerous questions. Sinta put a little extra power into her charm spell to make sure it took hold, but he succumbed readily enough. He denied, with some indignation, that either he or the envoy had any involvement in the poisoning of Lord Alfron, but he admitted that the courtier's death had been convenient, providing as it did an opportunity to advance Lord Torvil's cause by positioning one of the baron's associates close to the throne.

Sinta pressed him to explain why Lord Torvil's fortunes should be of such interest to the County of Menfir.

Thogril smiled. "Torvil aims to bring down Thennis, who is no friend to Menfir. Thennis is the glue that holds together the League of Three Principalities, the alliance between Sildoor, Fendoran, and Ool. Remove him, and the League will soon splinter—especially if the new chancellor is someone like Torvil, who is sympathetic to our interests and will do whatever he can to make that splintering happen."

Sinta knew the chief purpose of the League was to safeguard the independence of the three principalities against the geopolitical ambitions of the Count of Menfir. "So, Lord Torvil would subordinate Sildoor's foreign policy to a foreign master. Why? I know his wife has property in Menfir."

Thogril obligingly went into the details. Apparently employing somewhat dubious methods, Lady Irolte's father, the late Second Baron of Griffol, had significantly extended his landholdings within the county—without, however, being able to add them legally to the territory of his barony. Having little affinity for his son and heir, he had upon his death bestowed these supplemental but rich estates instead upon his daughter. The count was now offering to create from those lands a new barony, to be named Ferigol, and to create Lord Torvil its First Baron, so that Torvil could style himself, quite euphonically, the Baron of Ferigan and Ferigol—assuming, of course, that he delivered what Thogril termed "the goods," after becoming chancellor of Sildoor.

"And did the count extend this offer in writing?" demanded Othir.

"Oh, yes, indeed. I was charged with delivering it to Torvil myself."

"You said that the prince wouldn't let us interview anyone of gentle birth unless there was substantial evidence against them," Sinta reminded Thennis afterward, "but Thogril has now thoroughly implicated Lord Torvil in treason." She briefly recapitulated the interview. "May we speak with him now?"

Thennis thought for a moment. "I will take it up with His Serene Highness."

⚜

Sinta and Othir remained in the chancellory to consume an excellent supper and await developments. Thennis was absent for a protracted period, but he greeted them with a grim smile upon his return and announced that the prince had authorized the arrest of the various conspirators. About an hour later, Master Siv and two hefty guards escorted the baron and his wife into the side-chamber in which Sinta and Othir had been conducting their interviews. Thennis and Ghelnor joined them.

"This is outrageous, Thennis!" blustered the baron, a tall, thin man with a cruel face and a pointed beard. "I demand that you release us immediately."

Thennis shook his head. "I think not, Torvil. You have been detected in your treasonous accord with the Count of Menfir, and the outlook for you is correspondingly bleak. I have brought you here to give you a chance to confess freely and perhaps to obtain thereby a less heinous punishment. Should you choose not to do so, I shall direct the sorceress Sinta here to use her magicks to compel you to tell the truth."

Lord Torvil spat angrily on the floor. "And what legal weight would such a confession have? If this person is a sorceress, no doubt she can ensorcel me to say whatever she wishes, regardless of the truth of the matter."

Thennis nodded. "You are, of course, correct, but should you choose not to submit to such an interview, the alternative is for us to subject you to the more traditional methods of Master Siv." He indicated the executioner, who responded with a gruesome grin. "Although I would imagine he, too, could compel most men to say whatever he wished them to, such, alas, is the state of our laws, that any confession he might extract will be treated as dispositive." He waved a dismissive hand. "But in any case, if—as we are reliably informed—you possess documents establishing your guilt, and we recover same, your confession, or lack thereof, becomes nothing more than a legal nicety. We would prefer to have it, but we will unfailingly convict you without it." He turned to the fashionably plump baroness. "All of this applies equally to you, my lady. If your role in this treason is in fact a less culpable one than your husband's, it would be very much in your interest to allow Mistress Sinta to elicit the truth from you, for I very much fear that Master Siv, by contrast, may not be content until he has extracted a more incriminating testimony from you than the facts actually warrant."

Lady Irolte could see the logic of the old lawyer's argument. "Let your pet sorceress cast her spell," she said sullenly. "I took no part in treason."

Thennis turned to Sinta. "Proceed!" he said.

Sinta cast her standard sorcerer's charm, rather than the wizarding one she had been using to interview the servants.

"Were you aware of your husband's efforts to oust Chancellor Thennis?" she asked, touching the side of her nose.

"Yes."

"Were you aware that he was acting in collusion with the Count of Menfir, through the latter's diplomatic representatives?"

"Yes."

"Did you approve of your husband's actions?"

"Yes, I did."

"Did you take any active role in the conspiracy yourself?"

"No, I did not."

"Do you know who poisoned Lord Alfron?"

"No."

"Do you know who hired an assassin to kill the sorcerer Halifor?"

"No."

"Do you know who hired a criminal gang yesterday to kill Sir Othir and me?"

"No."

Sinta looked questioningly to Thennis, who asked, "Are you aware of a communication from the Count of Menfir, offering to create your husband Baron of Ferigol in exchange for subordinating the foreign policy of Sildoor to that of Menfir?"

"Tell the truth," Sinta instructed.

"Yes."

"Do you know where he keeps it?" Thennis continued.

"Yes, in a strongbox in our bedchamber."

Thennis nodded to Sinta. "That will suffice."

Sinta released Lady Irolte from the charm.

Thennis turned back to Lord Torvil. "And with that, my dear baron, I think the jig—as they say in the criminal underworld—is up!"

⚜

Lord Torvil grudgingly conceded defeat and confessed. He then submitted to Sinta's charm spell to clear himself of the poisoning of Lord Alfron and to clear his friends and children of complicity in the foreign conspiracy. Ghelnor drew up a protocol recording his confession and another recording Lady Irolte's. After the baron and baroness signed them, Master Siv escorted the guilty couple to the dungeon. Thennis decided that a night in the cells would serve Thigtonil, Donaril, Hrogan, and Fainor right, so he left them where they were. He then directed Ghelnor to retrieve a bottle of fine Esdiric brandy and four elegantly blown glass snifters from his office.

"I am grateful to you both," he told Sinta and Othir, "for exposing Torvil's little scheme. There may be diplomatic repercussions, but I don't think the count will dare make too much trouble over the affair. In addition to the League, some of his other neighbors have reason to distrust him. I think they would back us if it came to a conflict."

Ghelnor poured the brandy. Sinta, who did not much care for spirits, sipped hers politely, whereas Othir savored his with intense satisfaction.

Thennis smiled. "From one of the best vineyards in Esdiron. Aged for eight years in an oaken cask before it was bottled."

Sinta put down her snifter. "What will happen to the baron and his wife?"

Thennis sighed. "Torvil will certainly hang. Should Irolte escape execution, she will be banished from Sildoor. The barony will revert to the crown, of course, and all the couple's property in Sildoor will be confiscated. We won't be able to enforce that upon her lands in Menfir, so I imagine she will go there and live out her life in comfort."

"What about their daughter, Lady Tisvena, and her four brothers?" asked Ghelnor.

"With the loss of the barony," Thennis replied, "they will of course be stripped of their courtesy titles. Whether Tisvena is expelled from court will be up to Her Serene Highness. The sons, I suspect, will find it convenient to relocate to Menfir, especially the eldest, who can expect, whether sooner or later, to inherit his mother's lands there."

"And the lesser conspirators—Sir Thigtonil and his friends?" asked Sinta.

"Sir Fainor will be investigated for embezzlement, but the others will just lose their appointments and be expelled from court." Thennis smiled wanly and took another swallow of brandy. "It is, alas, no crime for them to disapprove of me."

The hour had drawn late by the time Sinta and Othir made ready to leave. Everyone was tired, especially the chancellor, but Sinta felt she had to bring up the point he had tactfully avoided mentioning. "Of course, we have yet to solve the mystery of who poisoned Alfron and arranged the murder of Halifor."

Othir groaned. "Time enough to worry about that in the morning!"

Sinta persisted. "I really should sit down and go through all of Alfron's old love letters, in case there's anything relevant there. And perhaps Your Excellency could arrange another pretext, this time to summon the Baron of Toth and his wife to the castle. We still need to talk with their servants."

Thennis chuckled. "Yes, I can see that you would, given Siguldina's history with Alfron."

Sinta gave a start at the name. "*Whose* history? And what history is that?"

Thennis looked at her with a touch of surprise. "Lady Siguldina's—the Baroness of Toth's." He smiled. "One problem with growing old is that events and scandals you take for granted turn out to have taken place before the people around you were even born. In this case, Lord Alfron left Siguldina at the altar and married Lady Hrinde, the daughter of a baron, instead. Of course, Siguldina had the last laugh, when she herself married an actual baron, and she was certainly better off without Alfron and his endless affairs. But she hated him for humiliating her like that—as well she might!"

Catching something of a second wind, Sinta pumped the weary Thennis for more information about the baroness. Much of what he could tell her tallied with what she already knew, but she extracted some new details, as well. Of common birth, Siguldina was a country girl from the

Kingdom of Listra in central Ondiran. Being reckoned a great beauty, and clever, too, she had made quite a splash upon her arrival in Talindor society some twenty-five years earlier. Thennis, however, had sensed no corresponding inner beauty. “It is nothing I could put my finger on, but something about that woman has always worried me.” Yawning, he raised a protesting hand to forestall another question. “But now, my dear, I must to my bed.”

17

Under no circumstances should the solution to the mystery turn upon magical or supernatural agency.

—*The Art of Mystery Writing*
(Ondiric Authors' Guild How-to Series, vol. 6)

After they returned to the apothecary's shop—accompanied by two members of the princely guard for added security—Othir marched resolutely to his bedchamber and went to sleep, but Sinta repaired to her study and stayed up until well past midnight. First, she retrieved a small book with snakeskin covers from her modest library. She had acquired it on a visit to the southern town of Lentiran three years earlier—at considerable expense given that it was written in a script she could not read. She opened it to the flyleaf, which contained the Ondiric inscription, "Siguldina, her book," in a style of handwriting fashionable some three hundred years earlier. "I thought so!" she murmured, after which she sat down, wrote a quick letter to Valdira, and teleported it away.

She then spent the next two hours carefully going through the contents of Alfron's wicker hamper, blushing occasionally at the content of some of the more indelicate love notes. She was nearly through them, without having found anything that struck her as important, when she came to a small bundle of three letters, fastened with a faded green ribbon. Each letter closed with a distinctive signum, a single character reminiscent of a serpent. On a hunch, she returned to the book she had consulted earlier and pulled from it a loose piece of parchment, covered on both sides with dozens of tiny characters in neat columns, written in the shiny, purplish black ink characteristic of the magic inkwell Sinta had bought at the same time as the book. "Aha!" she exclaimed, upon finding the character from the love letters on her list. "Gotcha!"

❦

Notwithstanding her late night, Sinta was up betimes the next day, and she had already worked her way through several tasty fruit-filled hotcakes when Othir joined her downstairs.

"This morning," she informed him definitively, "we shall go speak with Sir Rildan."

"The herald?" Othir sounded puzzled. "I thought we'd ruled him out."

"We have," Sinta confirmed, helping herself to additional hotcakes brought out from the kitchen by Ferga, "but he may have useful information."

❦

Sir Rildan was a short man in his mid-forties, with unkempt hair and a cast in one eye. He maintained a workroom in the great round tower, filled with heraldic clutter and dominated by a dusty banner depicting a rampant griffon in green and gold, left over from a tournament some years earlier. He confirmed that he maintained genealogical and heraldic records of all the Sildooric noble families, but if he thought it odd that Sinta should wish to know about the Baron of Toth and his wife, he gave no sign of it. On the contrary, Othir had the impression that he was flattered anyone—though perhaps especially a pretty young woman—might show an interest in his work at all.

It took a few minutes for Sir Rildan to find the correct bundle of parchments, for if he had a filing system, it had no apparent rational basis. Having once located the bundle, however, he cleared a space on one of his work tables and opened it up.

Sinta examined a colorful rendering of the family's coat of arms, depicting two mustelids of some kind, facing off, as if in battle.

"Gules, two martens rampant combatant sable, armed, langued, and pizzled or," explained the herald, as though he thought this would help.

Sinta praised the artistry, then looked over the family tree, which traced the different lines, some as far back as five generations. It was a less ornate production than the coat of arms, being for the herald's reference rather than display. Sinta saw that the Second Baron's name was Lord Saafinor and confirmed that his three children with Siguldina were named Caador, Terinifulte, and Anthilor. She pointed to the spot for the baroness. "Tell us about Lady Siguldina."

Sir Rildan scratched his ear. "Of low birth, of course, but very handsome." He shuffled through the parchments.

"If I'm not mistaken, my predecessor, Sir Poldar, made inquiries, when she married the baron. Lord Saafinor had just come into the title, I believe, and was perhaps the most eligible bachelor in Sildoor." He squinted, trying to make out the rather messy handwriting. "Let's see. Ah, yes, here we are. 'The lovely Siguldina, born in the village of Benth in the Kingdom of Listra. Only surviving child of the miller Leeth and his wife, Ugorisdina, also reputed to have been a great beauty.'" He shook his head in wonderment. "The names of some of these people!" (Sinta nodded, looking uncommonly pleased.) "Let's see, what else? 'Following the marriage, Leeth became quite indecently prosperous—'" He clucked his tongue. "Well, you know what these millers are like! '—and bestowed upon his daughter a dowry in the sum of 100 Listrian royal crowns.'" He gave a soft whistle of surprise. "That must be—"

"Over 120 Sildooric princely crowns," said Sinta, who was good with figures. "I can see why she was considered a desirable match—notwithstanding her 'low birth.'"

"We need to speak with His Excellency," Sinta told Ghelnor, upon reaching the chancellory with Othir. "I believe I know who poisoned Lord Alfron."

Hastening into the chancellor's office, Ghelnor soon returned to usher them in. Thennis rose courteously from behind his desk. "I understand you have news."

Feeling suddenly nervous, Sinta took a deep breath, as she sought to order her thoughts. "Yes, Your Excellency, I believe we do. From the beginning, we have had any number of suspects who might have wanted to kill Lord Alfron, but none who possessed a demonstrated capacity to carry out the specific crime we had before us. I am now convinced, however, that the Lady Siguldina, who hated Lord Alfron and also had reason to hope his death would work to the advantage of her son, and who left the banquet hall in time to circle around and waylay the server Tarilor in the corridor—after what appears to have been a staged argument with her husband—" She paused, realizing that her sentence had become unwieldy. "I have become convinced that she does have that capacity, that she is, in fact, secretly a witch, who could not only magically poison the prince's pork tenderloin, but also tamper with the server's memory, so he would have no recollection of the event."

Thennis raised his eyebrows. "And your reasons for believing this?"

Sinta paused again, for just a moment, as she tried to decide how best to convince him. "I do not claim to have definitive proof, Your Excellency, merely a strong suspicion. You told me once that you do not trade in rumors but in established facts. Unfortunately, with regard to witchcraft we are largely dependent upon rumors, for established facts are few and far between. Nevertheless, the combination of established facts and likely ones seems to me to point unambiguously to Lady Siguldina.

"Of all the magical traditions, witchcraft is the one about which the least is known—less even than about necromancy, whose illicit practitioners have good cause to be secretive. The reasons for our lack of knowledge, I believe, arise chiefly from the largely rural character of witchcraft, in contrast to the highly urban character of the other traditions. Although its mystical language does have a written form, relatively few witches can read or write. Witchcraft is thus a primarily oral tradition, passed down from mother to daughter—again in contrast to the other types of magic, which rely heavily upon the written word to preserve more spells than any individual sorcerer or wizard can remember. As a result, there is a correspondingly much smaller supply of written witchery available for outsiders to study. Moreover, while townsfolk have become more accustomed to—and tolerant of—magicians, the ignorant peasantry remains mostly afraid of magic, resulting in occasional outbursts of persecution directed against witches, who thus have every incentive to keep their identities and practices secret."

Thennis coughed. "While this is—genuinely—very interesting, Mistress Sinta, perhaps you could get more directly to the point?"

"Forgive me, Your Excellency. I meant only to illustrate the potential significance of Lady Siguldina's origin as a miller's daughter, from a heavily rural part of Ondiran, where she would have been raised to keep her identity as a witch a closely guarded secret." She paused, rather apologetically. "Of course, I do realize that the overwhelming majority of country girls are not in fact witches, but please bear with me." She tidied away a stray lock of hair that had fallen over her eyes. "Much of what we know about witchcraft is based upon rumor and guesswork, but it should not be surprising that witches seem to have a more intimate connection to the natural world than do magicians of the urban traditions. They are, for example, said to be able to control the weather, to cause sickness in cattle and poultry, or to choose the sex of an unborn child. They are also reputed to have a spell that turns food poisonous, without having to brew and introduce a separate poison, as sorcerers would have to do. Such a spell would have been extremely efficacious in the present case, for it would have contaminated the entire pork tenderloin, guaranteeing that Lord Alfron would be poisoned upon tasting it, whereas a toxin merely added to the meat might easily miss the morsel he chose to sample."

Thennis nodded, though he continued to look skeptical.

"Witches," Sinta continued, "also have a reputation for hexing people who offend them. I therefore found it significant that servants here in the castle have what otherwise might appear to be a superstition regarding unpleasant things that happen to people who anger Siguldina—apparent coincidences such as breaking out in pimples or being kicked by a mule. It has occurred to me to wonder if Siguldina took a silent measure of revenge upon Alfron and Hrinde many years ago, by cursing their infant son, Frildar, to grow up to be a profound disappointment.

"Moreover, witches are also said to have a spell to make their unborn daughters extremely beautiful when young, albeit at the cost of becoming hideously ugly in old age, and Siguldina was a great beauty, as was her mother before her."

"Her daughter, Lady Terinifulte, is also quite lovely," admitted Thennis, "though it would hardly be unusual for an attractive couple like the Baron and Baroness of Toth to bring forth attractive offspring."

"Of course, Your Excellency," Sinta acknowledged. "None of this evidence, so far, is more than vaguely suggestive. I did not, in fact, have more than the merest suspicion that the baroness might be a witch until last night—when I learned from you that her name was Siguldina." She opened a satchel she had brought with her from home and took out the small book with snakeskin covers. "Three years ago in the Duchy of Hriss, I happened upon this volume, a rare work written in the mystical language of witchcraft." She opened it. "And here, on the flyleaf, a previous owner has written in an old-fashioned hand, 'Siguldina, her book.' I consulted my former teacher, Lady Valdira, who has access to a reference collection far beyond my own, and she confirmed my suspicion." Taking out a parchment that had arrived that morning before breakfast, she read:

> You are quite correct in surmising the existence of a famous witch after whom both your baroness and the previous owner of your book might have been named. During the Time of Troubles, the original Siguldina succeeded in overcoming the popular prejudice against witchcraft to such an extent that she was accepted as the leader of a fierce peasant uprising in central Ondiran that nearly toppled the existing order in Thindon and Listra, as well as sparking smaller revolts in parts of Rohliran and Fothiran. When her movement was brutally—and perhaps inevitably—suppressed, she evaded capture and disappeared, becoming the stuff of legend.

Sinta handed the parchment to Thennis to see for himself. "Furthermore, this morning we learned that Siguldina's mother was named Ugorisdina. I did not have to consult anyone to know that she had been named for an even more famous witch, the supposed founder of the entire magical tradition over a thousand years ago. Under the circumstances, I wouldn't be surprised if it turns out that the baroness's daughter, Terinifulte, also bears the name of a notable witch."

"That certainly seems possible," observed Thennis, who was now looking rather more impressed than he had previously.

Sinta took the bundle of three love letters from her satchel. "Here is what I consider significant further evidence: three old letters to Alfron that I believe were penned by Siguldina." She undid the bundle and showed Thennis the squiggly signum closing each of the letters. She took up her book again. "When I first obtained this volume, I spent quite some time studying it. Although I couldn't read the text, I decided to figure out whether each character in the script represented a different word, as with some western languages, or a different syllable, as with the mystical languages of sorcery and thaumaturgy, or a different individual sound, as with the languages of wizardry and necromancy—or for that matter with Ondiric, Esdiric, and Tseren. I established that it was in fact a syllabic script, for there were nowhere near enough unique characters for each to represent a different word, but also too many to represent individual sounds." She showed Thennis the small sheet on which she had copied out the different characters in tidy columns. "Here you can see that the woman who wrote those letters to Alfron signed herself using one of the glyphs from this book. Given its serpentine appearance, I would speculate it stands for the initial *si* in Siguldina. If that is correct, it would represent an example of something akin to what I believe scholars term onomatopoeia: a serpentine symbol having been chosen to represent a sound similar to the hissing of a serpent."

Thennis nodded. "Interesting. Yes, Siguldina could well be guilty. The question is, how do you propose to prove it?"

Sinta bit her lip. "For the moment," she replied, a trifle uncertainly, "I think our best hope is that the servants implicate her. Failing that, perhaps we can either charm or bluff her into confessing. Or, a search of the baronial castle at Toth might uncover incriminating evidence."

Thennis looked doubtful. "Perhaps, but merely proving that she's a witch does not establish her guilt regarding the murders. Still, let's see what the servants have to say."

Thennis decided to sit in on the interview. Both servants made an extremely proper impression. The baron's valet, Baldir, was a tall, sandy-haired young man with an aura of the utmost competence, while the baroness's maid, Norilte, was an older, no-nonsense sort of person, with sharp eyes that missed nothing. Given what Sinta had heard about their employers, she surmised that only superior servants could hold onto positions in the baronial household at Toth for any length of time.

Disappointingly, neither one knew who had poisoned Lord Alfron. Baldir opined that it was shocking that anyone should attempt to murder His Serene Highness—though it was fortunate the attempt had been thwarted by the prudent employment of a taster, albeit at the cost of Lord Alfron's life. Presumably, it was the work of levelers or similar malcontents, who should be hunted down and subjected to an exemplary punishment.

Did the baron and baroness discuss the poisoning?

Baldir acknowledged that they did. "It is most improper, however, for servants to repeat what they inevitably overhear in the course of their duties."

Sinta nonetheless prevailed upon him to do so.

"Her ladyship expressed satisfaction at Lord Alfron's decease," he said, frowning.

"My mistress disapproved of Lord Alfron," explained Norilte in a more helpful tone.

"In reply, his lordship laughed," Baldir continued, "and said that perhaps Lord Anthilor would now have his chance at last."

"They are both most concerned for Lord Anthilor," Norilte said. "He has always had difficulty living up to the example of his older brother, Lord Caador, who is such a model Ondiric nobleman."

Othir inquired about the couple's spat in the banquet hall, but neither servant was aware of the incident.

"Her ladyship returned early from the meal," Norilte admitted dubiously, "but she did not seem in any way out of sorts. On the contrary, I thought she seemed in good spirits."

"Nor did they quarrel when his lordship returned later with the news about Lord Alfron," said Baldir. "No, I think you have likely been misinformed, sir, by some perhaps malicious person. It is rare for the master and the mistress to be at odds. They are a most devoted couple."

Changing topics, Sinta asked about the murder of Halifor.

Both servants denied overhearing any discussion of the killing, either before or after the fact. They certainly had not overheard anything about hiring an assassin. The very idea was shocking. Baldir expressed the view that such an assassination, carried out by night within the castle itself, was an attack upon the sacred order of things—even if it had been directed against a low-born sorcerer.

When Sinta asked, however, if either the baron or his wife had done any traveling between the two murders, Baldir admitted they had taken a brief trip to Faldot in the Duchy of Mar-Faldot.

Sinta and Othir exchanged glances, and Othir gave Chancellor Thennis a quickly whispered explanation of the significance of Faldot, as a place where the assassins' guild maintained an active presence.

His lordship, Baldir explained, had some business affairs to attend to there. Norilte added that she and her mistress had spent most of the visit with a particularly skilled dressmaker.

What about two days ago, Sinta asked. Had anyone from the household visited Talindor?

Baldir acknowledged that the master had absented himself for most of the day, apparently on some private errand. It was possible he had gone to Talindor, for the journey back and forth between Toth and the princely seat was not arduous. Why, just the day before that, for example, Lord Caador had visited home for no more than the afternoon.

Asked if she knew anything about the baron's errand, Norilte could say only that she had seen her ladyship give his lordship a ring of some kind before he left. He put it in his pocket. Norilte assumed he was taking it to a jeweler for repair.

"Did either of you know," Sinta asked abruptly, "that Lady Siguldina was a witch?"

Baldir scoffed. "What an idea! Who *have* you people been talking to? A witch, indeed!"

Norilte rolled her eyes. "Of course, I knew she was a witch. I've known that for years." She gave Sinta a look, as if to add, "Men! They don't see what's right under their noses, do they."

Pressed for details, Norilte could tell Sinta little of substance. Her ladyship had not confided the secret to her. Rather, Norilte had worked it out on her own. "It was obvious, wasn't it? A country girl like her, for whom everything always goes well, while going badly for those she doesn't like." She gave Baldir a supercilious look before returning her gaze to Sinta. "Witches are supposed to have their own mystical language, aren't they? Well, I heard her muttering something strange just before an insolent servant fell off a ladder and broke his wrist. And then there was the night a neighbor, who'd angered her, lost three sheep to a wolf—a wolf, here in Sildoor!" She hesitated, suddenly appearing less imperturbable. "Also, once, shortly after I came into her service, a groom from the stables sought to have his way with me. When I told her ladyship, she said: 'Never you mind, Norilte. He won't ever try *that* again!' And the very next day, his lordship's prize stallion kicked the boy in the head and left him simple-minded."

"Your mistress seems a vindictive woman," commented Sinta.

"She believes in retribution," replied Norilte evenly.

Sinta asked about the daughter, Terinifulte. What sort of a person was she? Did Norilte have any reason to think that she had learned witchcraft from her mother?

"Perhaps," the maid conceded. "Well, yes, I would assume so. But their ladyships have never gotten along." Her expression softened slightly. "Lady Terinifulte is a sweet, gentle girl, but she has always known her own mind, and the mistress often had to punish her for being willful."

"And what is Terinifulte's relationship with her two brothers?"

"Oh, she is devoted to Caador. I think she feels sorry for Anthilor, but they are not close: he finds it hard to forgive her for being clever and beautiful, not to mention brave enough to stand up to their mother, when he is none of those things."

18

Witchcraft mania—of which there were only sporadic outbursts during the medieval period—became an alarming feature of the early modern era. Encouraged by official campaigns to suppress supposed magic use, the superstitious peasant population raged against alleged witches and wise-women, resulting in numerous gruesome deaths.

—*Witch-Hunting in Early Modern Ondiran*

"I must congratulate you," Thennis told Sinta after dismissing the two servants, "for correctly deducing Lady Siguldina's involvement in witchcraft." He smiled wryly. "Of course, it remains for us to prove that she used her esoteric knowledge to poison Lord Alfron."

Sinta did not dispute this. "We have not yet proven that she commissioned Halifor's murder, either," she pointed out. "And now that we know the baron and the baroness both went to Mar-Faldot, I think it's likely that he was the one to hire the assassin—to protect her—just as it appears that he was the one who paid the gang to attack Othir and me, wearing a magic ring given to him by his wife. It wouldn't be surprising, if they're really so devoted to one another."

Thennis nodded. "That has certainly been my impression of them."

Sinta took out her wand and toyed with it as an aid to thought. It was a delicate instrument, made of fragrant sandalwood. "I wonder," she said after a moment. "Yes, I should have thought of this before. There may be a way to establish who carried out the poisoning. It's unlikely to work, but it's worth a try."

"You have our attention," said Thennis.

"It is always unwise," Sinta observed (sounding, Othir thought, a little like Valdira in one of her more didactic moods), "to assume that someone else, in a given situation, will necessarily do what you would do yourself. Or, indeed, that they *can* do it." She put the wand back in her pocket. "If I needed a memory spell, for example, to prevent someone from implicating me in a poisoning, I would choose one that irrevocably wiped the incident in question from the other person's mind. Attempting to dispel such a casting is no more effective than dispelling a magical fire *after* it has consumed a piece of parchment. The memory, like the parchment, is still gone. The wizarding charm, for instance, that I have been using on the servants operates in this manner. And, in all probability, Siguldina used a spell of this type to wipe the memory of the server, Tarilor, after she poisoned the pork tenderloin. But not necessarily. Not all memory spells are the same. Some just block a person's access to the memory without destroying it, in which case, dispelling the enchantment enables the mind to reach it again. We know nothing about what sort of memory spells exist in witchcraft. These blocking spells may be all that witches have ever learned to do. Or blocking spells may be all that this particular witch ever learned to do. Therefore, we need to speak with that good-looking young server again (preferably *after* a tasty lunch), to see if I can unblock his memory."

❦

An hour later, Tarilor was surprised and apprehensive at being summoned to the chancellory, of all places, since Sinta's wizarding charm had left him with no recollection of having gone there five days earlier.

"Don't worry—you aren't in any trouble," Thennis assured him kindly. "We just want to hear what you know about the day Lord Alfron died." He walked the boy through his story. Once again, Tarilor was puzzled at his inability to remember walking down the connecting corridor. Thennis explained that the sorceress Sinta was here to try to help with that.

Taking her cue from the chancellor, Sinta sought to reassure the boy, whose nervousness had visibly increased upon being introduced to a sorceress. There was nothing to fear, she told him. The spell she would cast would not hurt. It might very well fail altogether, but if it worked, it should get them to the truth about Lord Alfron's murder.

Tarilor steeled himself, as if for some mighty ordeal, and Sinta cast her remembering spell on him. "Now, think!" she urged. "What did you see when you left the kitchen?"

His eyes widened with astonishment, as the memory flooded back to him. "Why, there was a woman in the corridor! She was blocking my path to the banquet hall. So I said, 'Excuse me, milady,' and she said, 'Is that for the prince?' And I said it was, and she said, 'Good!' And then she reached out and touched the pork tenderloin and murmured something. I didn't think she should do that! So, I said, 'What're you doing, milady?' And she said: 'Never you mind, boy. Now, don't keep the prince waiting.' Then she touched my forehead, and everything went a little fuzzy for a moment, and I forgot all about her and went into the banquet hall and handed the platter to Lord Alfron."

Sinta beamed. "That's excellent, Tarilor! This woman, you didn't recognize her?"

"I don't know her name, but I've seen her here in the castle before. Nice looking, she is—for her age anyway—and always dressed like a very fine lady." He paused to remember. "Dark blonde hair, and strange eyes, sort of a golden yellow, like a cat's."

Sinta looked to Thennis, who nodded. She turned back to the boy, who still looked like he could not quite believe what had just happened. "Thank you, Tarilor," she said. "You've identified the murderer." She gave him a confidential smile. "I'm sure Pavia and Rovina will be impressed!"

In the discussion that followed, Sinta and Othir favored arresting the baronial couple without delay, but Thennis preferred merely to bring them in for questioning. There was not yet sufficient evidence, he explained, to arrest Lord Saafinor, and the arrest of Lady Siguldina needed to be handled with care, given how dangerous she appeared to be. For security, he sent for his bodyguard, Fothenar, as well as the executioner, Master Siv. The latter was to bring along his "magician's collar," an enchanted band of steel and brass that rapidly drained away the spell power of the wearer, rendering that person unable to perform magic.

After Thennis obtained the prince's permission for the interview, Ghelnor located the baron and baroness and escorted them to the chancellory on a pretext.

Notwithstanding a few gray hairs, Lord Saafinor was indeed a handsome fellow, tall, dark, and well-built, with little sign of the expanding waistline that often comes with middle age, while Lady Siguldina, with her remarkable amber eyes, was undeniably striking, even if a close inspection of her face would have revealed the first signs of the degeneration into a hideous old crone that was the price of the enchantment her mother had cast upon her in the womb.

Saafinor slipped a protective hand around his wife's waist, as he surveyed the unexpected occupants of the improvised interview room. "What's the meaning of this, Thennis? Who are these people, and why have you summoned us here? It's obviously not for the reason this mendacious minion of yours gave us."

Thennis, who had risen politely upon their entrance, made a placating gesture. "My apologies, Saafinor. Under the circumstances, I'm afraid deceiving you was necessary. You and your lady wife are here, at the prince's command, to answer certain questions regarding the murders of Lord Alfron and Court Sorcerer Halifor, as well as a murderous attack upon the sorceress Sinta, here, and her man-at-arms, Sir Othir." He sat down again.

Saafinor scoffed. "What nonsense! We know nothing of any of that."

"I hate to contradict you," said Thennis pleasantly, "but the evidence indicates otherwise." He motioned to Ghelnor, who brought in Tarilor.

"That's the woman I met in the corridor!" the server exclaimed, pointing, without waiting to be asked.

Siguldina put up a good front. "Who is this boy? What corridor? What mad delusion is this?"

Sinta stood up from behind the writing desk she had been using to take notes throughout her interviews. "This is the boy who saw you poison the prince's dinner by witchcraft in order to kill Lord Alfron—the man who once jilted you—in the hope of advancing the career of your son Anthilor. I have dispelled the memory block you placed upon him. He now remembers everything."

Siguldina looked stunned for a moment, but her husband came to her rescue. "Piffle!" he exclaimed, glaring at the sorceress. "Thennis, this woman and this boy must be in league together to slander my dear wife for some underhanded purpose."

Thennis shook his head. "I think not, Saafinor. She has conducted this investigation at my behest and under my direction. It has led to your wife, and to you, as well. Or do you deny play-acting the quarrel between the two of you in the banquet hall?"

Sinta broke in before the baron could answer. "And what about your trip to Mar-Faldot, to protect your wife by commissioning an assassin to slay His Excellency's first investigator, my dear friend Halifor, before he could uncover the truth?"

Siguldina had by now regained her equilibrium and seized upon a tactical error on Sinta's part. "There the false accuser betrays her purpose," she exclaimed. "She's desperate to fix the blame for the loss of her 'dear friend' on someone, anyone—and my husband and I are convenient."

Sinta looked ready to make some heated retort, but Thennis gestured for her to hold her tongue. "No, my lady," he told Siguldina firmly. "I can attest that Mistress Sinta's investigation has been most methodical, displaying no signs of desperation." He rose from his seat. "Lady Siguldina, it is my solemn duty, in the name of His Serene Highness, Prince Folgar, puissant ruler of the Sovereign Principality of Sildoor, to arrest you for murder and your husband, Lord Saafinor, Second Baron of Toth, on suspicion. Master Siv?"

The executioner stepped forward with the "magician's collar."

In a display of greater speed and agility than Sinta would have expected from a man in his late forties, the baron drew his sword and slashed open the advancing executioner's femoral artery. Siv gave a sharp cry and fell bloodily to the floor, dropping the metal collar, which rolled under the chancellor's chair. Fothenar, drawing his own sword, stepped forward to interpose himself between the baron and Chancellor Thennis, whom he was sworn to protect.

At the same time, Siguldina threw what undoubtedly would have been a highly unpleasant hex at Sinta, but the amulet the sorceress had taken from the assassin in Torul absorbed the magical energy of the spell, leaving her unharmed. With a cry of frustrated rage that merged into a lupine snarl, the witch turned herself—clothing and all—into a well-grown tawny-gray she-wolf and lunged at Sinta. Distracted by the baron's attack upon Siv, and caught off guard by the sight of a woman transforming instantaneously into a ravening beast, the sorceress barely had time to conjure up an invisible barrier to protect herself, but Othir—who had drawn both his sword and the assassin's dagger at the first sign of trouble—got there first. Notwithstanding the continuing disinclination of either weapon to obey him, he succeeded in skewering the on-coming wolf, thrusting the dagger through its throat and the sword deep into its chest. The wounded beast crashed into Sinta's magical barrier, while the momentum of a hundredweight of hurtling wolf threw Othir painfully up against it, as well. Both combatants sank to the floor, where Othir did his best to worsen the animal's already mortal injuries. Its yellow eyes gleaming ferociously, the creature kicked and struggled, as it sought desperately to rend Othir's flesh with its claws and teeth before dying, but without success.

With Siv rapidly exsanguinating on the floor and near death, Fothenar advanced to engage the baron. Being half Saafinor's age and in peak physical condition, he should have enjoyed a significant advantage, but the baron's blood was up and he fought well. Indeed, it was he who achieved the first hit, a flesh wound to Fothenar's left arm. At this point, Othir was still struggling to free himself from his entanglement with the bloody carcass of the wolf, so Sinta intervened in the battle instead, by casting a spell to put the baron into a deep sleep, as she had done with the thug Bogir. Fothenar—not realizing what had happened and seeing his opponent suddenly stagger and lose his footing—seized the opportunity to stab and kill him.

Thennis, who had retreated with Tarilor to the relative safety of the doorway to an adjacent chamber, stepped back inside and surveyed the carnage. "Well," he said softly, "I did hope that would go rather better."

19

The role of the court magician will vary according to the dictates of his sovereign. Some rulers will require that he devote most of his attention to military matters, others to civil engineering projects, still others to the preparation of lavish entertainments. A few magicians with a talent for divination have proved useful as key advisors. But whatever is required of him, the court magician must always keep in mind that his core function is to bring glory to his sovereign, whether by enhancing the latter's renown among his peers or by inspiring devotion among his subjects.

—*The Art of the Courtier: A Practical Guide to Courtly Behavior*

One week after the unpleasantness in the chancellory, the newly appointed Sorceress to the Court of the Sovereign Principality of Sildoor was surveying the appalling clutter in her new workshop high in the round tower. Creating order out of chaos would require time and effort, but Sinta knew it would be worth it. Though she had chosen to continue living above the apothecary's shop, the tower's well-equipped workroom would bring her to the castle on a daily basis. An air-purifying spell had mostly eliminated the mysterious metallic odor, and she had begun to sort through Halifor's belongings, mingled as they were with those of his predecessors. Sinta had little interest in spending time at court (though Shingach's cooking was a draw), but the professional opportunity was not to be gainsaid.

Fortunately, the prince seemed likely to make few calls on her services, beyond expecting a top-notch pyrotechnic display at the annual Vendritan harvest festival. Chancellor Thennis would probably require an occasional spell or two, but Sinta could hope she would otherwise be free to pursue her research into the world's several systems of magic, now with the aid of a generous salary. With satisfaction, she looked over to Angvar, who was sprawled in the windowsill, enjoying the morning sun.

For his part, Othir, the newly appointed Protector of the Court Sorceress, was sprawled more artistically, but no less languidly, on an upholstered bench from which he had displaced a faded map, a pot of writing quills, a sweat-stained smock, and two precariously balanced glass beakers containing noisome and potentially hazardous liquids. So far, his official duties, which consisted of thwarting any further murderous attacks upon Sinta, had not been onerous, while his unofficial ones, which consisted chiefly of entertaining her with cynical commentary on the prince's court, he found thoroughly enjoyable. Also, the pay was better than hitherto.

This morning he was recounting the latest scuttlebutt, according to which the court's Zoorist chaplain—to the delight of his Asardian, Hrintic, and Cantiferian counterparts—had been detected in an indiscretion with a footman, notwithstanding his vow of celibacy. Having little interest in celibacy himself, Othir sympathized, but he did not expect things would end well for the man. "If you have a taste for footmen," he opined, "it seems foolish to enter the Zoorist clergy, which so firmly disapproves of such liaisons."

"Hmm," replied Sinta noncommittally, as she tried to decide whether a shattered magnifying lens was beyond magical repair. Concluding that it was, she placed the glass shards in a large sack of material she would be consigning to the castle's rubbish heap.

A knock on the door brought Othir to his feet, as he retrieved his weapons from a nearby work table. While he considered the danger of a murderous attack on Sinta to be low at this point, he preferred not to see one attempted while he was unarmed and helpless. Fortunately, the two magic blades were now fully reconciled to his ownership. Killing something with them seemed to have been the key.

Sinta opened the door with a wave of her hand. She did not usually indulge in this sort of showy magic, but she thought a certain amount of theatricality was probably expected of the court sorceress.

A beautiful young woman entered. She had her father's dark hair but her mother's remarkable amber eyes, and she carried herself with a poise and grace that Sinta had never quite achieved—though admittedly the visitor's elegant attire contributed to the effect.

Hoping that Othir had not been underestimating the danger of murderous attack, Sinta slipped a hand into the pocket containing her wand. "Lady Terinifulte?"

The witch's daughter gave a skillful curtsy. "Court Sorceress Sinta. Sir Othir."

An awkward silence followed. Terinifulte examined the walrus skeleton by the door. "What manner of beast was this?" she asked at last.

Sinta explained what little she knew of walruses and their ways.

The visitor nodded. "Someday I would like to travel to the sea," she said, a trifle wistfully.

Sinta let go of the wand but kept her hand in her pocket. "It is worth visiting," she acknowledged, "but I don't personally recommend sailing upon it any more than necessary." Sinta's experiences with seafaring had been mixed.

Terinifulte took a few steps further into the workshop and ran a finger tentatively along the rim of a copper cauldron. "The reason I have come," she said, "is to let you know that I bear you no ill-will. Chancellor Thennis has conveyed the particulars to me, and in all honesty I cannot see how you could have acted other than you did."

Sinta breathed a little more easily. "That is a generous attitude for your ladyship to take."

Terinifulte considered this point of view for a moment. "My mother would have agreed with you, but she would not have found it praiseworthy. She had no concept of forgiveness." Her aristocratic self-possession faltered for a moment. "It has been the challenge of my life to forgive her for that."

Sinta, who had never known her own mother, felt a wave of compassion for this young woman, whose filial-maternal bond had been so fragile. She invited her to sit down and offered her a cup of *noriboth,* an Ondiric herbal infusion that was held to be particularly soothing.

Terinifulte took a seat on the padded bench and watched Sinta conjure up a tiny fire atop a tiled work table and perform the simple ritual of the infusion's preparation.

"How do your brothers feel about the matter?" asked Othir, discreetly positioning himself between Sinta and their quiet but still potentially homicidal guest.

Terinifulte regarded him steadily. "Well, I know Caador feels a bit guilty about mentioning to our parents that you two had taken over the investigation. He never suspected them of the murders, so it never occurred to him that they might try to have you killed." She considered Othir's broader question further. "Caador was closer to our father than I was, and I think he is perhaps a little overwhelmed at inheriting the barony sooner than anyone expected, but he did remark to me that our parents, by choosing to die fighting, spared us the humiliation of witnessing a public trial and execution. And Chancellor Thennis has been very kind about containing the scandal, as well as encouraging His Serene Highness to appoint Anthilor to be a Gentleman of the Chamber in place of Sir Thigtonil." She paused a moment to reflect. "I don't think Anth really knows how he should feel about it all. My little brother is always in a bit of a muddle, when it comes to anything more complicated than dressing himself, or eating the food others have prepared for him." She smiled tenderly. "But luckily that shouldn't get in the way of dressing the prince or tasting his food. Or being his friend. He'll certainly be better at those things than he was at managing the kennels."

Sinta brought over Terinifulte's cup of *noriboth.* Handing it to her, she could sense the girl's innate magical power, mingled with the pleasant scent of rosewater. "They really gave us no choice, you know."

Terinifulte sighed. "I know. I'm afraid my parents didn't believe in giving other people choices. They considered choosing to be solely their own prerogative." She breathed in the aroma of the hot *noriboth* before taking a cautious sip and deciding to let the scalding infusion cool a little.

Sinta retrieved a second cup for Othir and poured a third for herself. "So, presumably she gave you no choice about learning witchcraft?"

Terinifulte gave something between a snort and a laugh. "None whatsoever. Mind you, it *was* very interesting. And there is something exhilarating about wielding the power of magic, as I'm sure you can attest yourself. Unfortunately, my mother used spells mostly to punish people."

"Including you and your brothers?"

"Especially my brothers and me." She hazarded another sip of *noriboth.* "This is really very good."

Sinta smiled. "My father was an apothecary. He taught me the best method for brewing it." She risked a sip herself and burned her tongue. "Tell me, did she also teach you to read and write the witches' script?"

"Of course. Right from the beginning. Before she taught me to read Ondiric. When it came to my magical education, my mother was very determined."

Sinta refrained from eagerly rubbing her hands together, but only with difficulty. She walked over to a shelf holding several volumes and took down the small book with snakeskin covers. "The woman who instructed me in magic was also very determined. Although a sorceress, she taught me a good deal of wizardry, as well, and even a little defensive necromancy. And in the years since, I have made a preliminary acquaintance with thaumaturgy. But of witchcraft I know next to nothing." She handed the book to Terinifulte. "I wonder, would it be asking too much of you to teach me?"

About the Author

Sedigitus Swift is a historian by day and a pseudonymous fantasy author by night (as well as during eclipses or otherwise under cover of darkness). When not diverting himself by writing offbeat medieval fantasy novellas, he specializes in the perplexities of modern Central and Eastern Europe. No doubt he has other equally perverse interests, but we are not currently certain exactly what those might be.

If you have enjoyed this book, you might consider subscribing to his engaging monthly newsletter, *The News from Ondiran,* at www.sedigitus.com, for advance word on upcoming works, insights into the creative process, and choice bits of Ondiric lore. It's free!

And if you're feeling really benevolent, you might leave favorable online reviews anywhere such reviews congregate. They don't have to be long or detailed, but they will help other readers find this book.

www.sedigitus.com

www.ingramcontent.com/pod-product-compliance
Lightning Source LLC
Chambersburg PA
CBHW030022060826
49398CB00031B/183

* 9 7 8 1 9 6 1 8 5 2 0 5 1 *